BEACH PULP

AMAZING STORIES SET IN REHOBOTH, BETHANY, CAPE MAY, LEWES, OCEAN CITY, AND OTHER BEACH TOWNS

NANCY SAKADUSKI, EDITOR
J. PATRICK CONLON, ASSOCIATE EDITOR

Cat & Mouse Press
Lewes, DE 19958
www.catandmousepress.com

Published by Cat & Mouse Press
Lewes, DE, 19958
www.catandmousepress.com
ISBN: 978-1-7323842-2-4

Cover illustration by Joe Palumbo
Cover illustration Copyright © 2019 Joseph Palumbo
Printed in the United States of America

ACKNOWLEDGMENTS

Beach Pulp was a bit of a departure for us, so I am hugely grateful to the guidance provided by my associate editor, Patrick Conlon, who educated me, reached out to new (to me) communities of writers, and even brought in our first graphic short story. Patrick helped me choose the stories, develop the cover, and identify sales avenues for the book. I also benefited from the experienced eyes of the genre readers, Dennis Lawson, Christopher Lyons, and JM Reinbold, who generously gave their time to help evaluate the stories we received. I would also like to thank Joe Palumbo, whose cover illustration pays homage to the old pulp magazines and perfectly captures the spirit of this book. And, as always, I owe much to the support of my husband, Joe, and my mermaid friend, Cindy Myers. –N.S.

Working with Nancy Sakaduski and Cat & Mouse Press has been an amazing experience. I couldn't have asked for a better publisher and am honored to have been made an official part of the Cat & Mouse family. I want to thank JM Reinbold and all the members of the Written Remains Writers Guild for their continued camaraderie and guidance throughout my creative endeavors. I also am eternally grateful for the friendship and support from Steve Myers and all my friends/partners at Oddity Prodigy Productions, without whom I could not have done this. Finally, and most importantly, I want to thank my wife Marcella Harte, who is my alpha and omega, and the reason I am able to write these words. –P.C.

Like the Cover?
See more of Joe Palumbo's art: www.joepalumbo.net

CONTENTS

MISSING IN REHOBOTH

BY JAMES GALLAHAN

This is the fifth year in a row that I've gone back to the place where my normal, everyday life ended. I shouldn't keep going back to Rehoboth Beach—to the same house we rented that summer. But I can't help myself. It's crazy, I know.

All my friends tell me to stop putting myself through it. They're right, but something deep down inside keeps bringing me back here. Maybe I'll find a clue I missed—a clue the police missed.

Sarah would be eight now. Ted would be thirty-five. We would have been married ten years.

After Sarah was born, we spent the first weekend each August at a house we rented on Wilmington Avenue. The house was just right for our young family. It didn't bust our limited budget and the beach was within walking distance. We ate at Grotto every night.

The night it happened is fixed in my brain. Ted took Sarah down to the beach for one more look at the ocean at night. They left at eight thirty. It was late for Sarah, but she loved to look at the moon. "It looks bigger here than at home," she'd say. Plus, we were on vacation, so…

I stayed back at the house and finished packing. Ted said they'd be back in forty-five minutes, so I started to wonder what happened when an hour and a half had passed. I figured they had just lost track of time. I locked the front door of the rental and headed to our favorite spot on the beach to look for them. I thought I'd join them and appreciate the sand between my toes before I had to go back to my job in the concrete maze—Crystal City, Virginia. But the beach was empty except for an elderly man fishing.

"Have you seen a man and a young girl?" I asked.

"Sarah and Ted?"

"Yeah, how'd you know?"

"The little girl was holding her father's hand and pulling him toward me."

"Yeah, that's our girl."

"She said her name was Sarah and her daddy's was Ted. What a cutie pie. She thought it was neat that I was fishing at night. I think your husband thought your daughter was asking too many questions, so he took her farther down the beach. They stopped to talk with a man and woman and then left with them—looked like they were heading for Brooklyn Avenue."

I furrowed my brow. "That's strange."

"Hope everything's okay."

"Maybe I just missed them on their way home."

I half-walked, half-jogged down Brooklyn Avenue, hoping to see them. No luck.

Why would they take Brooklyn Avenue? That's not the way home. And who were the people they were with?

I didn't hear any noise as I walked up the sidewalk to the house. Usually, Ted has music on or Sarah is watching a *National Geographic* show. Smart for her age, she seemed to absorb information like a sponge.

I unlocked the door and saw that they weren't in the living room. Calling their names, I ran upstairs to the bedrooms, but they weren't there. My chest tightened. I tried Ted's cell phone again. No answer. Now my heart was pounding.

It had been two hours since they left to go to the beach. If Ted had taken her to get ice cream or something, he would have called to let me know. That was our rule. We always told each other where we were going and when we'd be back.

I called the police, trying to explain what happened between sobs. They arrived at the house in five minutes. Sergeant Williams stayed with me while two other officers went to the beach.

Williams pulled out his notepad and pen. "Mrs. Patterson, are you having problems in your marriage?"

"What? No. We're happily married."

Williams continued to write in his notepad. "Sorry, ma'am. Have to ask. These two people you say your husband and daughter left with, do you know who they might be?"

"No. I have no idea."

"What's your husband's cell phone number?"

He jotted it down, frowning, then started to walk away. "We'll be in touch, Mrs. Patterson. Please let us know if your husband and daughter come back or if you hear from them."

I sighed and clenched my jaw. "Thank you, officer. I will.

You've been a *huge* help."

Williams turned around and narrowed his eyes. "Good night, Mrs. Patterson."

That was five years ago.

I never really understood when people said that it's the not knowing that tears you up inside. Now I get it. Maalox and Xanax are my best friends these days. If it weren't for them and years of therapy, I probably wouldn't be able to talk about what happened without breaking down. Of course, I wish that Ted and Sarah would just walk through the door and everything would be like it was. If not that, then I wish I knew what happened. Was it something I did? Was Ted mad at me? Who were those people on the beach, and did they have anything to do with it?

So, here I am at the same rental house, on the same week-end, five years later. Each year, I go to the beach around eight thirty at night and stay for an hour or so. I can't help thinking maybe they'll show up. You know—like some *Twilight Zone* episode. Maybe they'll pop up on shore after being in a time warp. It's stupid, I know, but I have to hope for some kind of miracle.

I head back to the house around nine o'clock and decide to watch a rerun of *The Big Bang Theory*, with my customary bottle of Coca-Cola and bag of microwave popcorn next to me.

I freeze when I hear a soft tapping at the front door. My heart races. Nobody I know would stop by at this hour.

More tapping.

I unhook the pocket-sized canister of pepper spray from my keychain and hold it with both hands, so it won't shake so much. Slowly, I slide the window curtains aside. *That's strange.* A little girl is standing on the front porch.

I shake less when I see the child, but my breathing doesn't slow down. Who knows who could be hiding out there. I speak from behind the curtains. "Can I help you?"

"Please let me in," a voice comes back, barely above a whisper.

Beads of sweat form on my forehead. "Are you all right? Where are your parents?"

No answer.

I crack the door open and scan the yard. No one. Just the little girl standing there on the front stoop, shivering, looking down at the ground. I put the pepper spray in my pocket and open the door wider. "Come in. I'm calling the police." I pull out my cell phone. Dead. I try the landline. Same thing.

I bend down. "What's going on, sweetie?"

"Father is dead," she says in a monotone, looking out the window. "He tried to run away. They shot him."

"What?" I look outside again. No one. "Who shot your father? Where is he?"

She stares directly at me for the first time and in a soft, even voice says, "He was running away from the testers. They shot him. I'm very smart. That's why the testers took me."

I stumble back. Her eyes are completely black. No color at all. I can't stop looking at them as I feel for my chair to sit down. "Uh ... What's your name?"

"The testers call me 714299. Father called me Sarah."

I lose my breath for a second. "Testers? What're you talking about? They call you a number?"

"714299 is my name. Father talked about you all the time."

"Your dad knows me? Who is he?"

She hands me a crumpled photo. It's a picture of Ted and our then three-year-old daughter, Sarah.

"Where'd you get this?"

"From Father."

Could this girl be my Sarah? No. Those eyes. Can't be. Were they abducted? Think. Think.

She glares at me. "We need to leave now."

"No. I'm calling the police." I slap my cell phone several times on the palm of my hand. "Why isn't this phone working?"

"The testers are coming. I don't want to make them mad."

"Stay on the couch," I say, eyeing the autographed baseball bat hanging on the wall.

I walk over and reach for the bat, accidently knocking it to the floor. I crouch down to pick it up and suddenly feel her standing behind me. She swings the Coca-Cola bottle before I can get my hands up. Stars explode behind my eyes—then everything goes dark.

I wake up with my hands and feet chained to a gurney in what looks like a hospital room. Figures move around me in a haze. Each is wearing a doctor's mask and surgical gown.

Most have those same black eyes.

Sarah leans over me, inches from my face. I can't bear to look at her lifeless eyes.

"What are you doing to me?" I ask her. "Get me out of these chains."

"Father said we'd be together someday."

"Ted's still alive?"

"Oh, no. He's dead. Father grabbed me and tried to run away but I bit him and ran back to the testers. I like being here with them. The testers always teach me new things. They say I am their best subject. But Father hated what they were doing to us. When he died, the testers told me to get you. A parent's blood is always needed."

I look at her, searching, trying to make sense of it all.

Sarah puts her hand on mine. "Don't worry, Mommy. Their experiments don't hurt *too* much."

James Gallahan has had short stories published in the January 2019 *Pilcrow and Dagger* literary magazine, *The Survivor*, and the 2019 Greater Lehigh Valley Writers Group anthology, *Rewriting the Past.* He was a finalist in the *Writer's Digest* May 2018 Your Story competition and won the Grey Wolfe Publishing's June 2018 monthly writing contest. James is currently working on a historical fiction/adventure novel based on the infamous king of pirates, Henry Avery. James lives in Virginia. You can follow him on Twitter @JG_Books.

CALL AGAIN

BY DENNIS LAWSON

I prefer to work alone, but that wouldn't wash in Bethany Beach. As one of Delaware's "quiet" beaches, Bethany is full of families, romantic partners, and groups of friends escaping their spouses. A guy like me—forty-something with permanent six o'clock shadow, pasty skin, and a receding hairline (with no family to account for the hair loss)—would stick out and arouse suspicion. I had a job to do that night, and the only way I could do that job was to blend into the crowd like an everyman. Which was why I'd brought along one of my associates from the organization—Holly, a forty-something herself, who was much better preserved and nicely drew attention away from me.

We were sitting on the second-floor deck of the Ropewalk restaurant, looking at the people going in and out of shops on Garfield Avenue or making their way to or from the beach. It was before noon, and the lunch crowd was sparse. I closed my menu. "It's a little early for a whisky sunset, but I'm going to have one anyway."

Holly lowered her menu just enough to reveal her sunglasses. She had long, lush, silver-blonde hair that curled at the end. "Tsk, tsk," she said. "You know my rule."

"What rule?"

"I don't know. Doesn't that sound like something a wife would say?"

When I asked her to come along and provide some cover, she said she wanted to play a married couple. "I get paid to have torrid affairs," she said. "If I'm going on vacation, I want to be married." Which meant I had to borrow wedding rings, plus an engagement ring, from a pawnbroker I knew. I couldn't wait to get this gold band off my finger. Meanwhile, Holly seemed to be enjoying her rings too much. I knew she wouldn't give them back.

"What are you getting to eat?" she asked.

"The burger."

"Get an appetizer too."

"Why?"

"Because I'm getting mozzarella sticks, and I'm going to eat all of them, and I don't want to look like a pig. Now listen to your wife."

She was wearing a black knee-length cover-up that was roomy enough to be decent over a two-piece red swimsuit and well-fed curves, along with thin cork sandals that had a bit of lift in the heel. I was also dressed casually, in a T-shirt, swim trunks, and old sneakers. We had gone to the beach earlier that morning, and while I went swimming, she worked on her tan. My swim trunks were still dripping.

"I think all that sun exposure did something to your brain," I said. "It's not good for you."

"Isn't that a shame? Things that are fun are so rarely good for you."

"But you don't worry."

"Darling. Worrying would give me wrinkles."

More people trickled in for lunch. Mainly families and twosomes. While Holly and I were eating, a lady who was sitting alone caught my eye.

She was farther inside, away from the deck, even though there were still plenty of tables over here. Apparently, the view didn't matter to her. She was a blonde in her thirties, pretty, with more makeup than she needed. Blue blouse, white capris, sandals. Under her table, there was a beach bag filled to the brim, with a towel bulging out on top.

Her glass of water was untouched. Her menu was closed, but none of the waiters seemed to be in a hurry to go see her. Her red lips were pressed together in an angry expression.

"Checking out the other merchandise?" Holly asked.

"What do you make of her?"

Holly shifted her gaze toward the blonde woman. "I'd bet a large sum that she's waiting to meet someone she doesn't care for. I've only been in that position a million or so times."

As if on cue, a man emerged from the stairs and crossed the room toward the blonde. The man was in his sixties, with a ring of gray hair around his head and a beige fedora on top. He wore a red Hawaiian shirt, khaki shorts above the knees, and boat shoes. He carried a brand-new beach bag very similar to the blonde's, possibly the exact same model.

I knew the man's name, Ned Grandon, because I was supposed to kill him that night. I had a solid report on his typical day-to-day activities. The Ropewalk was his usual lunch spot. But I figured today's lunch was a little out of the ordinary.

Ned sat down and slid his bag next to the blonde's. They had a brief, seemingly unpleasant, conversation. Then the blonde grabbed the handles of Ned's bag and walked away.

"Hey, stick around," Ned called out. "My treat."

The blonde didn't answer and continued into the stairwell.

"Do you know anything about this?" Holly asked.

"Nope," I said through my burger. "I'm guessing he's collecting some money to try and save his skin. It's too late."

"I think we should help her."

"He's not going to be a problem for her anymore after tonight."

"But you'll have a loose end."

I wiped my mouth. I was curious, and Holly didn't look like she'd take no for an answer. "Take your purse and tail her," I said. "Make like you're heading for the bathroom."

Holly pulled her small purse out of the canvas beach bag under our table. Besides our towels and sunscreen, the bag held my Glock 26 with a small suppressor based on an old military design. There was also a burner phone, with another one in her purse.

"I know what I'm doing," Holly said. She stood up, put on her black straw hat, and gave my cheek two quick slaps. "You still owe me a dessert."

I signaled the waiter and paid the check. I had been drinking cola with my burger, with occasional sips of the generously tall whiskey sunset. I still had half the whiskey concoction left. I took a final sip, picked up the canvas bag and, with some regret, walked away.

At the bottom of the stairs to the ground floor, a framed cigar box label featured the face of a brunette with short flapper hair and green eyes. She watched me go. Below her cute but menacing face were red letters that spelled, "Call Again." Below that, in smaller letters, it repeated, "Call Again." There was something ominous about the message that made me hope I'd live through the day and be able to return.

Outside, in the bright sunshine on Garfield Avenue, I put on sunglasses and looked around the crowds. Holly stood only a block away, at the corner of Garfield and Atlantic Avenue, in front of Bethany Beach Books. She gave me a brief wave. A few feet from her was the blonde, now in shades herself, looking at nothing at all. Other people were gathering there too. It was a trolley stop.

"Your head is getting red," Holly said. "Should've worn a hat."

The trolley pulled up. It was more of a bus now, but the iconic look remained: a bright-yellow top half and a sky-blue bottom half emblazoned with "Bethany Beach" in yellow letters. The blonde got on first and took a seat in the middle. I followed Holly toward the back. She took the window seat.

The trolley headed north along Atlantic, parallel to the boardwalk and the ocean. The third stop took us near the Addy Sea, a well-known bed-and-breakfast in a Victorian house. "That's where we should've stayed," Holly said. We were staying in a nice but inexpensive motel about two miles south.

"Next time," I said.

Holly arched an eyebrow and smiled.

The trolley headed west, into a residential neighborhood. I

thought about Ned, who seemed pretty cheerful for a guy so far in debt to the organization that he had become a marked man. He was an accountant who was willing to help his clients in any way they could afford. But as his clients met a variety of ends, some pleasant, some less so, he tried to maintain his lifestyle with gambling. That works for some people, but not most. Ned was lucky he managed to hold on to his beach house in the divorce. He mainly gambled (and lost) at the organization's venues. The boss had been willing to float him some money so he could get back on his feet. But at this point, Ned owed too much for too long to keep breathing.

At the next stop, behind a family with kids, a guy about ten years my junior boarded. He made no effort to blend in—plaid sport coat over a white collared shirt, dark blue jeans with a wide brown leather belt, and brown loafers. Mirrored shades, and I could only guess at the large caliber of the gun he was sure to have holstered beneath the jacket. There was probably a gold watch under there too. He exuded enough confidence for everyone on the bus to choke on.

He sat down beside our blonde friend. I felt much worse for her, and for the first time, I was glad we'd followed her.

Everyone else on the bus was paying attention to their own groups or watching the town go by outside. Holly and I were the only ones reading the tension between the blonde and the schmuck. They exchanged a few words. The man leaned forward, and I guessed he was rifling around in the blue beach bag.

I reached into our bag and took my phone, wallet, a pack of cigarettes, and a lighter. I didn't like leaving the gun behind, but I wasn't planning on doing anything but tailing if this guy got off.

He did just that at the next stop, another residential area. "Stay on her," I said.

The good news was that the guy seemed indifferent to me, even though I was the only other person getting off. It helped that a lot of people got on there. I did some bad acting as I exited the trolley, taking a look at the time on my watch without seeing it, and gazing over at the church across the street like it had meaning to me. And then I walked in the direction of the plaid jacket, thirty feet ahead but as loud as ever. I didn't have to walk far. Mr. Plaid Jacket took out a pair of keys, ducked into a street-parked blue BMW, and sped away. Jersey plates.

New Jersey, I thought. *Of course.*

I sat down on a bench and had a cigarette.

A text came in from Holly. *Got off next stop. Followed. Off the Hook Restaurant.*

That was west on Garfield Avenue, about a mile walk from where I was. It was a much shorter walk to where my car was parked in a metered spot near the beach. Then I remembered that I had left my car keys in the canvas bag, a far too chivalrous gesture. I texted that I'd be there in twenty minutes.

Cars whizzed by in both directions. At least there were sidewalks. I felt the sun on my head, and thought about Holly telling me I was getting red. If I saw a gas station, I would duck in and buy a hat.

About fifteen minutes later, I came to a short row of restaurants, including Off the Hook and a nice Italian place. Across the street, there was a Wawa, a gas station, and a diner. The hat could wait.

The sign in front of Off the Hook said, "Fresh. Honest. Local." They weren't the sort of words that appealed to me. But I was pleasantly surprised when I walked in. Beyond the cozy rows of four-person tables, there was a small bar made of dark wood. Very inviting. The bar had six seats. Five were empty, and the blonde was in the sixth.

Holly was at a table at the other end of the place, with a menu and a strawberry milkshake. "So, what happened?" she asked when I sat down.

"He got into a car with Jersey plates and peeled out of here."

"What do you want to do?"

"Retire," I said. I asked the cute waitress for a black coffee. "I don't like the fact that Plaid Jacket was willing to go through this little drama to get something from Ned. I assume that Ned sold something valuable to the blonde and also to that guy, to maximize his profits. And this guy was willing to rob a woman in public to get it. What does Ned have that we don't know about?" My coffee came and I drank some. "We need some info from her."

"I'll go get her," Holly said, pushing her chair back.

I reached out and put a hand on her arm. "Just a sec. We need a plan that doesn't end with her testifying against me."

"Leave it to me."

Holly crossed the restaurant and joined the blonde at the bar. Less than two minutes later, the two of them joined me at our table. The blonde had a scotch, and Holly had a gin and tonic.

"This is Kimberly," Holly said. "She understands that she's going to forget everything about us and what we say, and we're going to forget everything about her. But we're going to help each other out, because Ned needs to be stopped."

Kimberly's anger had faded into forlorn sorrow. "Why not?" she asked. "My life is over anyway." She had more of her scotch.

"Whatever Ned gave you—which the man in the plaid jacket took from you—I intend to return to you," I said. "Just level with me, and after I give it back, forget me. That's all I ask."

"Why are you helping me?" she asked, tears in her voice.

"Because Ned is my enemy too. And because my friend here asked me to."

Kimberly put her hands over her face and composed herself. She took a deep breath. "It's like this," she said. "I used to live a different kind of life. When I was twenty-two, I was Ned's mistress. I was into all sorts of stuff back then. But I've turned my life around. I'm married, I have two kids, I'm a teacher, and my husband has no idea what I used to be like."

"Oh, honey," Holly said. "You should never have to apologize to a man for the life you led before you knew him."

"That's a great attitude, but I just don't want him to know. So anyway, he grew up loving Bethany Beach. We come here for two weeks every summer. I know Ned is around. One time, he gave me a leer and a wicked smile, but otherwise, it's been fine. The only problem is that, back then, he took pictures of me doing bad things. I always hoped he had moved on to other girls and didn't care about those old pictures. But then, out of the blue, he calls me up at our rental. He tells me he'll sell me the pictures for five grand, or he'll show them to my husband for free. Now I'm out five grand and someone else has the pictures."

"But why would this someone else want them?"

"I have no idea," she said a little too loudly. Holly patted her arm. "Sorry," Kimberly said.

"Did he get all the pictures?"

She shook her head. "No. I was looking at them when he came over on the bus and pointed his gun at me. You know, I wanted to make sure Ned had really coughed them up. I realized after the guy on the bus was gone that one had fallen on the floor." She handed it to me. "This one isn't anything explicit. A bunch of low-lifes were partying at the Hotel du Pont that night. Ned had his camera."

The first thing I noted about the dark photo was the date printed in orange: June 21, 1999. The next thing I saw was Kim in the foreground, holding a drink and looking as devilish as anyone I'd ever known. I looked up at her just to make sure it was really the same person. It was. And then I noticed in the background—a little blurry but still clearly recognizable—my boss, twenty years younger but still not all that young. Evidence that he was in Wilmington on the night of June 21, 1999, the night of three murders the local press had dubbed the Summertime Slayings. One Delaware man with no known ties to organized crime, though of course he had plenty. Two associates of a criminal organization in New Jersey. No good suspects. There had been whispers that it was Paul Cartwright, the man who would go on to be my boss, but he had plenty of witness statements to show he was at the beach at the time. In actuality he made his bones with those murders, and eventually rose to the top.

"Are there more shots of this party?" I asked.

"Yeah, a few."

"We need those photos," I said. "Do you know anything about the guy in the plaid sport coat?"

She shook her head. "I've never seen him before."

I closed my eyes and leaned back. "Leave your number with Holly and go home. We'll give you a call when we get the photos."

"How do I contact you?"

"You don't."

Ned Grandon had a small but nicely maintained one-story house on Delaware Court. Trees and bushes along the drive-way and around the house gave him some privacy. It used to be a beach house for him, but with his kids grown and his wife gone, this was his permanent residence. He didn't know it, but he came here to die.

It wasn't far from the restaurant. We crossed the street to the Bethany Diner, on the corner of Garfield and Half Moon Drive. We followed Half Moon down a few residential blocks, and there was the woodsy Delaware Court. I didn't see any blue BMWs, but there was a forest-green Jaguar in Ned's driveway.

"Yuck," Holly said. "My mother always loved Jaguars."

"Good luck," I said. I hung back while she walked up the driveway, beach bag in tow. All I had in my pocket now was my Glock with the mini-suppressor already attached. It was still small enough to fit in my bathing-suit pocket, if not exactly comfortably.

Holly rang the doorbell. The plan was for her to explain to Ned that she was a thank-you gift from the New Jersey fellas for cutting an honest deal. According to our recon on Ned, he took his dinners at Mango's, a great restaurant that overlooks the beach. He used to throw his money around to pick up ladies. Lately, he had been relying on his charm—and striking out. So, the odds were good that he would believe any story Holly laid on him.

The door opened and Holly talked her way in. A couple minutes later, I entered onto soft white carpeting in a lush living room: black leather couches, large-screen TV mounted on the wall, bright abstract paintings from the 1980s, a variety of plants, and a portable chrome bar, where Ned was fixing two drinks.

"Things are certainly going your way today, aren't they?" I asked.

Ned turned around, crystal bottle in hand. "And who the hell are you?" he asked.

"I'm here on the matter of your debt to the organization."

"I'm in one of their spots practically every day of the week. And they send a goon into my house like this? I'm insulted. I'll be in tonight, and I'll have plenty of cash with me. We can chat then. For now, how about you go catch a wave."

I sat down on the couch. I hadn't pulled my gun out because I thought Ned would talk more if he felt like he was in a position to negotiate. I was also confident that, if he had a gun anywhere nearby, I was still a faster draw.

"Ned, I saw the girl come in. I'm guessing you want me out of here as quickly as possible. I'll give it to you straight: We know you cut a deal with a New Jersey crew. We want them more than we want you. Tell me who the man in the plaid jacket is and where he's off to, and I'll be on my way."

"I don't know what you're talking about," he said, before draining his glass and shakily pouring some more.

"I'm not going to wait all day," I said. I didn't envy him. It wasn't an easy choice.

"No more debt," he said.

"What's that?"

"I'll tell you everything, but I want my slate wiped clean."

I sat back and acted like I had to think about it. "That's a tall order."

While Ned had himself another pull of whiskey, the front door swung open.

Speak of the devil, it was Mr. Plaid Jacket. "I knew something was up," he said.

Ned spit out some of his whiskey in surprise, right on that nice white carpet. "I told you not to come here!"

"Shut up, old man. Your setup was too weird. I hung around to see if my suspicions were right. Sure enough, two jokers from Old Man Cartwright's crew come waltzing in here."

"I don't know what you're talking about," I said. "The girl was booked to come here. I'm the cashier."

"Do I look like an idiot?" Plaid Jacket asked. "I know you're a triggerman for Cartwright." He pulled a gun out from under his jacket and casually pointed it at me. He said to Ned, "I'm pretty curious why he's on your couch and you're not full of bullets."

"What's taking so long?" Holly called out. "I'm still waiting for my drink." She walked in, stark naked, and leaned her arm on the wall. "Who the hell are you?" she asked Plaid Jacket.

His mouth was still falling open as I drew my gun and fired two quick shots into his chest. I dove to the floor and got him twice more, one high in the chest and one in the head. He didn't manage to get a single shot off. He dropped and started bleeding.

Ned backed away from the body straight into the wall. He was shaking, so I guided him over to the couch and sat him down.

"I need my heart medicine," he said. "In the bedroom."

"I saw it," Holly said. She left and came back with a glass of water in one hand and pills in the other. "Open your mouth," she said, jamming the pills in there. She brought the glass to Ned's lips, and he took it away and drank. She got the whiskey, but Ned shook his head no. She lightly slapped his cheek and forced the booze on him. "Grow up," she said. He took a few swallows, then let out a hacking cough.

"Oh, God," Ned said. "You know, it's funny. All these years, I had no idea what I had. I have lots of pictures of girlfriends. Kim just happened to be someone who was nearby and had the means to be blackmailed. When I dug up those old photos, I couldn't believe it when I saw Cartwright in them, and on that night. I didn't even know who he was back then. It felt like a goldmine. I could touch Kim for some easy cash, and then I figured the New Jersey guys would love to take Cartwright down. They could give the photos to the police, leak them to the press, kill him themselves. But the way things worked out, you saved my skin as much as you saved your own. You name your price, it's yours."

His speech took some effort. He laid down on couch.

"Why go through the trouble of including Kim?" I asked.

"You guys think you're so smart," he said. His eyes were closed, but he was speaking normally. "I think I noticed someone tailing me a couple times. I figured I was under surveillance. No way did I want to be seen with someone from another..." He trailed off. He was asleep.

"What'd you give him?" I asked.

"His heart medicine. Maybe a little more than the recommended dose. The thing is, it has nitroglycerine in it. You can't mix that with the little blue pills that a lot of my customers like to use. So, it's unfortunate that he had one of those, too."

"What's going to happen?"

"He'll go into cardiac arrest pretty soon." She walked out of the room. "I'm getting dressed," she said.

Once Holly was ready, we carried Ned's body to his bed. The five thousand dollars that Kim gave him was on his bureau. His body spasmed a few times while we were in there, and that was that. We left the fellow from New Jersey dead on the living room floor.

We found the blue BMW farther up the street. Kimberly's photos were on the passenger seat. I took the photos and we walked to the Bethany Diner, where we finally had a full meal, plus dessert. Then we took the trolley back to where my car was parked. My meter had expired, and I had a ticket.

Once we were back in the motel room, it was time for some phone calls. Kimberly made an excuse to her family and dropped in to watch us burn the photos, since we obviously couldn't just return them. She didn't ask for the five grand back, which was good, since I knew the boss would want it.

I called the boss and told him about the day's adventures. He was very pleased, to say the least. I had some money coming my way. Also, he agreed to send some associates to Ned's house to clean up and dispose of Plaid Jacket and his car.

I told Holly I was going to the Ropewalk for another whiskey sunset. "Want to come?"

She was on the bed wearing her black cover-up and watching television. "I have an appointment tonight."

"Really? You're working?"

"I mean, you can cut in if you can match my price," she said, smiling but not bothering to look at me.

"You know I can't afford you. Especially since I'm splitting my payment for this job with you."

"Now that's what I wanted to hear." She turned the television off and swung her legs off the bed. "Let's go."

"What about your appointment?"

"Didn't you hear? I'm on vacation. I earned it."

Dennis Lawson is an adjunct instructor at the University of Delaware in the English Department. His fiction has appeared in *Philadelphia Stories,* the *Fox Chase Review,* the crime anthology *Insidious Assassins,* and the Rehoboth Beach Reads anthology series. Dennis holds an MFA in Creative Writing from Rutgers-Camden, and he received an Individual Artist Fellowship from the Delaware Division of the Arts as the Emerging Artist in Fiction in 2014. He lives in Newark, Delaware, with his wife and daughter. Learn more about his fiction at www.dennislawson.net

A MILLION TINY BITES

BY D. M. DOMOSEA

A sunny beach. A comfortable lounge chair. And an easy pulp read.

Now if only Stacy would leave him alone, the day might be worth the trouble it took to wake up.

Ryan felt her eyes on him, studying him, forming yet another criticism. He could practically hear the words banging against each other as they linked together in her mind, like train cars on a single-minded track, building the necessary steam to come barreling out of her mouth. Their destination: his vexation.

He returned his attention to the book, hoping she'd leave him alone. He'd purchased the paperback at one of the Cape May shops, an impulse buy displayed on the counter near the register. It was an anthology of light summer reads titled *Beach Pulp*. He'd read through the first two entries—a *Twilight Zone* sort of story and a noir detective tale—before settling in for the third story, a supernatural horror called "Night of the Killer Coquinas." It had a satisfying Koontzy-King vibe.

"How's the new book?"

Ryan winced. The question was measured to sound casual.

An unassuming and friendly handcar dispatched to test the conditions of the track before sending out the locomotive. The trick was to find an answer with balance. One that conveyed he was not purposely avoiding conversation yet was invested enough in the paperback to not invite further discussion. He paused and placed his finger mid-page.

"Hmmm ... not bad. Surprisingly well-written and compelling." He risked a quick glance in her direction, an obliged acknowledgment. He couldn't read her eyes behind the dark, oversized sunglasses, but her mouth formed the lopsided smirk he detested. The one that said, "We both know you're full of shit."

She nodded and tilted her head to look past him. A child not of their making—thankfully they had not visited that folly upon themselves—sat scooping out sand from her small section of the beach, creating a toddler-sized crater. Stacy appeared interested in watching her, so Ryan returned to his book. He reread the last sentence to ground himself:

The coquinas require an incapacitated victim, for they are numerous and ravenous but very small, after all.

"Maybe I'll read it when you're done. If you think it'd interest me."

The engine was powering up, brakes releasing for the initial lurch into motion. It was best he not give it fuel, but with Stacy, that could be anything he said or did. He answered with a simple nod and grunt of agreement. Stacy fidgeted in her lounge chair, dissatisfied with his response.

Bubbles of laughter erupted to his left. The child scooped up lumps of sand with her tiny hands and studied them, threw it all down, and scooped up another mound, doing the same. After a few more cycles of scoop-and-dump, scoop-and-dump, Ryan realized she was watching bean clams—coquinas—burying themselves back down into the shallow sandbanks in her palms. Her happiness was so simple and basic, so pure.

How irritating.

How one goes from the innocence of joyous childhood to the mirthless existence of maturity was a sad commentary on the human condition. His resentment of that fact, fueled by his wife ceasing to find anything redeeming about him these days, redirected his ire to an easy target: the child and her joy in the harmless, insignificant presence of those bean clams in her hands.

"Ryan, I want to talk—"

"Hey sweetie, what you got there?" Ryan put on his best kid-friendly face.

The girl looked up at him. A moment of hesitation passed over her delicate features before a smile bloomed across her face. She leaned over and grabbed two fresh batches of watery sand, ambled over and shoved her hands at him. At least three coquinas lay exposed, looking like little gray, purple, and orange pebbles. Two of them wiggled as they searched for cover in the thin layer of sand in her palms. The child giggled at their futile attempts.

"You know, I'm reading a story about those little things. They're called coquinas."

"Co-qui-nas," she repeated, testing each syllable.

"And it says that for each one you uncover and hold in your hand, thousands more lie hidden in the sand, just below your feet."

The child's eyes grew wide as she looked down at the beach beneath her shrimp-like toes. "Thousands?"

Ryan leaned in for the next part but made sure to speak loud enough for Stacy to hear. "And, it says that if you ever fall asleep on the beach at night, millions of them will come to the surface, latch onto your legs, your arms, and your neck, and cover you from head to toe with their tiny bites."

The girl shrieked and shook her hands free of the sand. Her eyes watered as she hopped from foot to foot and then took off back down the beach toward her parents, a sobbing mess.

"That was mean and unnecessary," Stacy growled.

The parents of the child comforted her and looked around the beach, slightly confused, before turning their gaze in Ryan's direction. He stood, threw his book into his bag, then grabbed his chair and gave it a couple of shakes to loosen the sand.

"I've had enough beach for today. Bring the umbrella when you come up, eh?" He turned and stalked up the dunes back to their Cape May rental, leaving Stacy with her train of reprimands parked at the station of her disapproving mouth.

Stacy was absent for the rest of the day. He didn't know if she'd stayed at the beach or toured the Washington Street Mall, but he didn't really care. The front door squeaking closed woke him from his nap in the guest room. Her steps paused outside the door before continuing to the master bedroom. The sound of the shower followed soon after.

Ryan checked the clock on the dresser. Six thirty. She'd been gone for a while, then. He reached for the book splayed out next to him, where he must have dropped it as he fell asleep. He found the spot where he'd left off—the coquinas swarming their final unconscious victim:

And the coquinas had their feast, a million tiny bites at a time.

One hour and another story later, the smells of dinner cooking drew him out from between the pages. He supposed it was time for a détente, or so his growling stomach said. Ryan made his way to the kitchen. The table was set for two and the wine glasses filled with a fresh merlot—his favorite. She must have picked it up while she was out.

Stacy glanced up from the pan of sautéed greens and nodded to the setting. "Truce?" she asked, raising an eyebrow to emphasize the tentative nature of the question.

He nodded once and offered a shallow smile. "Yes, of course."

She plated their dinner and served him, wearing a look he interpreted as the smug peace of a minor victory. He picked up his wine glass and took a hearty swig. The velvety red was pleasing to his tongue.

"Mmm … good choice."

"Thank you," she replied, a larger smile filling her face. "Picked it up at a small winery on Railroad Avenue."

He finished the glass, and she poured him another. If he played this evening right, he might get lucky with Stacy for the first time in … over a month? Two months? He'd lost count, but he'd had other options, ones he pushed from his mind so as not to distract from the opportunity at hand.

The rest of the meal passed in a mundanity of polite but thin conversation. He talked about his company's recent departmental reorganization while she droned on about vaccines and new safety protocols at Fort Detrick. Nothing of true meaning or consequence was shared but the evening was made bearable courtesy of the merlot. He filled his glass for a third time as Stacy nursed her first glass through the entire meal. It was good wine—he felt it in the tingle of his fingers and toes.

As the last of his third glass reached his belly, Stacy sat back in her chair and cleared her throat. *Shit, here we go,* he thought.

"Ryan, I think it's time we talk." She stared at the half-finished food on her plate and nudged her wine glass around on the table. "About last summer."

Ryan stiffened. Stacy must have taken his silence as consent because she continued, her voice louder and emboldened.

"About what happened while you were in Palma …"

"Palma was a business trip. Meetings all day. Networking at night. You saw my agenda—utterly boring. There's nothing to talk about."

"Yes, there is." She looked up at him. Her fingers stopped pushing the wine glass and instead tensed around the base of the stem. "You know there is."

Ryan's heart pounded heavy and fast in his chest. *Did she know?*

Ryan stood and grabbed the bottle of merlot as he stalked past her.

"Don't run away from this, Ryan. Where are you going?"

His answer was the sound of the screen door as it slammed shut behind him.

The beach was empty. It was almost ten and just past peak season, so their private section of the New Jersey shoreline was deserted. Under a waning moon, the sand gleamed like a bright ribbon stretched out between the row of summer rentals and the dark blue of the night-capped ocean.

Ryan picked a spot next to a set of wooden pilings that marched out to the water in two rows. He plopped down a couple feet away, heavy from the effects of nearly an entire bottle of wine. He took another deep swig to wash away the bitterness in his mouth. The alcohol by volume must be high for a merlot. The tingling sensation in his fingers and toes spread now through his limbs, into his shoulders and down to his hips. He hoped it would soon numb his mind as well.

What did Stacy know, or think she knew? She had no proof; he'd been too careful for that. Covered his tracks. Only corresponded at work. Coincided rendezvous with legitimate business trips and plausible meetings. She couldn't know—not with any certainty. Still, the mood of their marriage changed after his return from Palma. A toxin festered between them for a year, and now—now—she wanted to confront him about it.

He wasn't ready for what would follow—the crying, the anger, the blame, the disappointment. That one bothered him the most. Not tears or rage but the self-righteous sense of her disappointment in his failure as the perfect husband. An unflawed husband. A faithful husband. Things he could now never be. He resented her for that disappointment, that unspoken critique of his worth as a man.

He finished the last of the bottle and made to throw it out

into the water but found it difficult to gain momentum with his arm. In fact, he struggled to lift his forearm past his chest.

Strange. His entire body felt ... strange. Heavy and clunky, and burning with the feeling of pins and needles, like a lightning storm striking inside every inch of his flesh. This was not the usual grogginess of too much wine. Something was wrong.

He startled when Stacy appeared, looming over him.

"Oh, Ryan. If only you'd been a better person, I wouldn't have to do this."

His pulse raced, and his entire body flushed with an unease that sped through his veins like fire. *If only? Do this?* Her words were more than just wistful sentiment. They were a threat.

"What? What did you ..." He tried to push himself to standing with his arms, but his legs failed to respond. He toppled over, as his body collapsed under him. The side of his face caught the sand.

"What did you ..." he repeated. The gritty beach filled his mouth and muffled his rage.

Stacy grabbed his arm and rolled him over onto his back. She kicked his feet out so his legs lay straight. He fought to reclaim his sitting position but found it difficult. It was as if his entire body was drained of all strength and function. Ryan spit the sand from his mouth and growled in frustration.

"I'm afraid it's no use, the struggling and straining."

"What the hell did you do, Stacy?"

She hopped over his legs and balanced with her right foot

on the first piling. It stuck out from the sand by only six inches or so, but she concentrated on the effort as if she were a hundred feet in the air. Ryan opened his mouth to scream at her, but she cut him short with an explanation delivered as flat and calm as the ocean before a storm.

"We've been working on a new pharmaceutical at Fort Detrick," she said, "an inoculation for nerve agents. One of the early formulas went far afield of what we were looking for. More a toxin stabilizer than a prophylactic, actually." She paused as she switched from her right to her left foot and rebalanced herself. "They deemed it a failure, but I thought it was an interesting little brew, so I smuggled some out of the lab. Just a couple of drops, and you lose complete musculoskeletal mobility. You won't be able to move for hours. Not until well past sunrise, I suspect."

A couple of drops? *Damn, the wine,* he thought. *Of course. That's why she'd barely touched hers.* Ryan didn't know what she was planning, but he guessed it wouldn't end well for him. Images of various tortures she might wish to inflict popped into his head. Buried alive? Dragged out to sea? Or—he gulped—subjected to a brutal castration? *God, no. Anything but that.*

"Help!"

Stacy grimaced at him and pulled a dinner napkin from the pocket of her shorts. He cried out a second time, but his throat constricted halfway through and weakened it to a pitiful yelp.

"None of that, now," she said. She hopped off her piling, leaned over him and stuffed the napkin into his mouth. "You have no one to blame for this but yourself, so take your punishment like a man. Like the deceitful, cheating man you are."

She turned her back on him and faced the ocean as her voice wavered. "You think I'm stupid and weak and willing to put up with your lies, your betrayals, but I'm not. Not anymore."

A sensation, barely perceptible, began to plague the entire backside of Ryan's body. Nips, tickling and itchy but not painful, shuddered in waves across the back of his calves and triceps. Maybe the toxin she'd given him was starting to wear off? Or maybe it was getting worse. Maybe his heart had finished pumping the poison throughout his entire body to do its evil work. Breaking down his muscles. His tendons. His nerve endings. Ryan strained to move his arms, his legs, his fingers and toes, but managed only the smallest of movements in each extremity. He whimpered through the cloth stuck in his mouth.

She spun around to face him again. "Oh, it's not lethal, you big baby. What do you think I am? Killing you isn't worth the grief of the aftermath." She smiled and leaned over him. "It's just time for a little harmless payback, that's all."

Then she set to work removing his clothes. She started with his water shoes, then moved to his T-shirt and shorts. She unbuckled his belt and yanked down the tan cargo shorts and boxer briefs together and with little patience. It might have been a turn-on, if the situation were different. If Stacy hadn't incapacitated him with her misappropriated toxin. If Stacy hadn't been Stacy.

Maybe he shouldered some of the fault for the breakdown of their marriage, but Stacy wasn't blameless. He'd only sought the attentions his marriage no longer provided, the affections his wife no longer gave. Whatever retribution or catharsis she sought in doing this to him, it didn't warrant this. He didn't deserve to be poisoned, to be assaulted in this way, and he'd be damned if he'd let her do it.

"Now, you'll experience everything I went through this past year, living with your deceit. The helplessness." She'd been standing near his waist on his left side but then side-hopped over him to his right in some celebratory jig. She kept her eyes locked on his as she spoke.

He had to move. Had to get away from this crazy bitch.

"The resentment." She hopped over his exposed groin, back to his left side.

Ryan concentrated on his legs. If he could just get enough feeling back into his legs.

"The loneliness and abandonment." She jumped over his thighs to land on his right.

Please.

Ryan begged his body—his useless lump of flesh—to move. Just one goddamned leg. Little pinches and twitches, too numerous to count or contemplate, prickled every inch of skin on his calves.

Please.

"And then, when the sun rises, and all the beachgoers swarm the shore and find you here, in all your glory, you'll be paralyzed with humili—"

Ryan's right knee jerked up and caught Stacy mid-hop. Too quick for her to finish her sentence or scream. Too quick for her to catch herself with her arms. She fell and hit the beach, with nothing more than a rough "oof" of air forced from her lungs at the impact.

For a few moments, the world around him fell silent. The sound of ocean waves, gone. The screeching of sleepless seagulls, gone. The taunts of his dangerously resourceful wife, gone. The momentary thrill of hope rushed in to fill the void. He'd done it. He'd moved! He'd beat Stacy's toxin. Now, for the other leg, and then maybe his arms would follow.

Ryan strained until his face was red, but his body betrayed him. He could move no further. He must have spent what little kinetic energy he had left in that one jerky movement.

Damn. Damn it all!

He turned his eyes—the only body part he still seemed able to move—to Stacy. He was at her mercy now. He mumbled as loud as he could through the napkin in his mouth, hoping to get her attention, but she just lay there. Stunned or embarrassed—he didn't care.

And then he noticed the pool of liquid forming beneath her head. A tide pool. It must be. One that wasn't there before? But no. He knew what it was. She'd hit her head on the piling she had balanced on earlier. The liquid was blood. The metallic scent of it filled his nostrils and made him gag. Ryan's entire underside, where bare skin met beach, bristled with an unsettling finality.

Dead. She was dead. His wife was dead, and he was now stranded and truly alone.

He was going to have to wait until someone came by and found them. A naked, paralyzed man sprawled next to a dead woman. How the hell was that going to look? Even with the gag in his mouth—hell, maybe because of it—this was going to look like some sick fetish fulfillment gone wrong. Or worse, one gone right. Ryan's best alibi was the toxin in his body. Hopefully, they'd be able to identify it and . . . a movement to his left caught his attention.

Stacy.

She'd moved. Her fingers or maybe locks of hair from a slight twitch of the head. Something. It was something, and it meant she was still alive. He focused on her moonlit form, searching for another sign of life. The sand around her wiggled and danced. Ryan exhaled heavily through his nose, relieved his miserable, vengeful wife was alive.

He continued to stare, waiting for her to sit up and hold her head.

Waiting for her to moan with pain.

Waiting for her to move.

Waiting.

But the more he watched, the more he realized that it wasn't Stacy moving. It was the beach.

Under the full moonlight, Ryan could make out shining, pearl-like bodies—no bigger than kernels of corn—latched onto Stacy's skin where it touched the sand. They covered the entire perimeter of her body, at least the parts visible to him.

He squinted, trying to make sense of what he was seeing. Were they bean clams? Yes. Coquinas, just like in the story he'd read earlier. There were just so many of them ... so many ... and they were swarming his dead wife. The tide pool of blood and brown hair around her head bubbled and rippled with hundreds of the tiny creatures.

He watched as the lower strata of clams sank back into the sand as a new wave crawled up and over those and latched even that much higher onto Stacy's skin. Ryan watched, transfixed, as this small movement played out over and over. One entire row of coquinas, likely thousands of them, nipped onto her flesh and buried themselves backward into the sand as another set crawled over them and did the same. Industrious little suckers. The sight was hypnotic, like one of those looping, spinning visual tricks that pulls you deeper and deeper into the illusion. Deeper and deeper.

Deeper and deeper, until his senses narrowed to the space in and around his body. What had been prickling annoyance earlier was now something more. A delicate pain that shimmered across his flesh, from his scalp to his roughened heels, accompanied by a gentle tugging, steady and insistent but slow. This was a result of neither the wine nor the toxin. Not a chill from the night air or the realization that his wife was dead.

This was the coquinas.

Just like in the story. Just like with Stacy. And he was helpless to stop it. Helpless to stop his descent into a grave carved by the creatures.

Their progress was tedious.

For they are numerous and ravenous but very small, after all.

Indeed, each one was no larger than the pinky nail on Stacy's now half-buried right hand. Even so, the feeling of sinking millimeter by millimeter into the ground terrified Ryan. The night dragged on as the quiet roar of ocean waves composed a soundtrack for Ryan's slow descent. The further into the sand the hungry little clams worked their prey, the easier it was for them to drag him under.

Where they would … they could …

Oh, God!

Tears streaked down Ryan's temples, making it only as far as his hairline before mixing with sand. Within minutes, grains of silica rasped the corners of his eyes, inflaming the soft white of his sclera so that he could think of nothing else but the discomfort. And at last, panic—true and terrifying—set in.

His mind screamed out orders to blink.

BLINK, DAMN YOU!

But all commands went unheeded. His flesh was nothing more than a cast. A prison created from the vagaries of a damaged woman and tampered wine.

The last of Ryan's sight succumbed to the harsh sand as grains spilled into his nostrils. A tug-of-war began between his attempts to blow the bits out of his nose and his sharp inhales to draw more air into his lungs.

It was a short struggle.

Before Ryan exhaled his fourth round of sand and snot, the tip of his nose—by far the greatest protuberance on his supine form—disappeared beneath the sand.

And the coquinas had their feast, a million tiny bites at a time.

🍷

D.M. Domosea is a certified adult for eight hours of the day and a universe creator for the rest. She is an active member of the Frederick Writers' Salon and has two stories in their self-produced anthologies, *Unlocked* and *Intersections*. She also writes a monthly column for the *Luna Station Quarterly* blog. You can find her on the web at www.dmdomosea.com or follow her on Twitter @DMDomosea.

THE CELESTIALS

BY PHIL GIUNTA

At Parsell Funeral Home in the quaint, coastal town of Lewes, Delaware, Laurel and Rodney Jaggar stood beside their sister's closed casket, shaking hands with a seemingly interminable line of complete strangers. Laurel was astonished that their reclusive sister, Celeste, had made so many friends since moving to nearby Rehoboth Beach eight years ago. It was only after the first dozen mourners expressed their condolences with such phrases as, "I loved your sister's novels," and "I met Celeste at a book signing at Browseabout," that Laurel understood the truth. These people were not friends, but fans. They knew Celeste only through her work and occasional public appearances. Nevertheless, their well-intentioned sympathies left Laurel with a bitter sting of guilt—neither she nor her brother had ever read a single one of Celeste's books.

As shame compounded her grief, Laurel wiped away another stream of tears and accepted the fact that these people probably knew Celeste better than her own family did. She shot a sidelong glance at the casket and closed her eyes, trying to erase the image of Celeste's battered body. Somewhere else in Delaware, the drunk driver who had taken her life was also being laid to rest.

Another loyal reader clutched Laurel's hand, muttered the standard cliché, and stepped aside. *Will this never end?* She sighed in relief as the last five people in line approached together, led by a distinguished, elderly gentleman with salt-and-pepper hair. He extended a hand and introduced himself as Rusty Dickinson.

"I can't tell you what an honor it is to meet you both," Rusty began. "I only wish it were under brighter circumstances. I know the past few days have been difficult for you, but we just wanted you to know that we owe a special debt of gratitude to Celeste. She helped each of us in ways no one else could, which is why we volunteered to be pallbearers."

Rod exchanged a wary glance with Laurel. "Well, uh, much obliged."

Rusty stepped aside and gestured to the others. The first was a tall, lean young man who introduced himself as Christian Bayard. As they shook hands, Laurel couldn't help but take note of his unblemished bronze complexion and square jaw.

By contrast, Virginia Kent was a full-figured teen with a leonine mane of raven hair that framed a sun-deprived face and complemented everything from her ebony matte lipstick to her one-piece black dress and thigh-high leather boots. *There's no way in hell our Celeste hung out with this chick.* Laurel could tell by Rod's forced smile that he was equally as disconcerted by the girl's appearance. *She looks like something that crawled out of the* Cabinet of Doctor Caligari.

Bringing up the rear was a nondescript middle-aged couple who introduced themselves as Dutch Draper and Carla Dodd. Doleful eyes belied their warm smiles as each engulfed Laurel and Rod in a firm embrace.

Laurel found herself wondering how such a motley group had ever come to know one another, let alone someone as reticent as Celeste. As if sensing her bewilderment, Rusty leaned close with a reassuring smile. "You'll understand everything soon enough."

The service was held at the Solid Ground nondenomination-
al church, where each of Celeste's friends delivered a brief,
touching eulogy. Virginia was the first to speak, addressing
Laurel and Rod directly.

"I want you to know how much Celeste helped me. I've
struggled with depression since I was really young, but I
started using X and other drugs after my family turned their
backs on me when I came out. Thanks to your sister, I've
been clean now for four years. I have an awesome job, an
apartment here in Lewes, and a new family that cares about
me. None of that would have happened without Celeste." With
a lopsided smile, Virginia wiped her eyes and stepped away.

Christian followed, recounting how Celeste had helped him
overcome his fear of the ocean after the drowning death of
his mother when he was a child. Then, Dutch and Carla took
the lectern together and credited Celeste with helping reunite
them after they'd lost touch nearly three decades ago.

Finally, Rusty Dickinson imparted a tale that left Rod
stunned and Laurel in tears. The murder of his wife six years
ago had launched him on a downward spiral into alcoholism.
Then a series of financial misfortunes left Rusty broke, home-
less, and on the verge of suicide. "But with your sister's help, I
found the hope and strength to take control of my life. I think
it's fair to say that Celeste saved me." He paused, spreading his
arms to indicate the others from his group. "She saved us all."

By the time they arrived at Henlopen Memorial Park, the
morning clouds had dispersed. Beneath an unblemished Sep-

tember sky, Rod and Laurel placed a teardrop-shaped bouquet of white pom-poms and lilies atop Celeste's casket while the others stood at a respectful distance.

"She deserved better from us," Laurel whispered. "We were the only family she had left, and we had nothing to say at her service."

She turned and stormed off toward Rusty and his group. "I'd like to know more about our sister and how she helped all of you."

Rusty nodded. "Well, no better time than the present. Have you eaten today?"

"Come to think of it, no."

"Let's do something about that. I'm hosting a reception later at my house on Delaware Avenue, not too far from Celeste's place. We'd be honored if you and Rod would join us."

As Celeste's sole heirs, Rod and Laurel had inherited her house on Sandalwood Street in Rehoboth Beach and were staying there for the week while they decided what to do with it. After freshening up, they walked the half mile to Rusty's place and were still discussing their options when they arrived.

"You should rent it out," Rusty advised as he poured drinks. "You could make a hell of a profit, pay off the mortgage, and have a vacation house when you need it. If you don't like the summer crowd, Rehoboth is open all year round. You should come here at Christmas—it's beautiful."

Rod shrugged. "I ain't much for the beach, but Laurel loves it." He nudged her with his elbow. "Maybe you'll finally find that rich husband you've been lookin' for."

She narrowed her eyes at him before addressing Rusty. "You

said that our sister saved your lives. Personally or through her writing?"

Rusty handed her a drink. "Both, my dear. I only wish I could have returned the favor." He addressed the others and raised his glass. "To Celeste. May her words last forever." Around the table, everyone repeated the sentiment as they clinked their glasses together.

Rusty pointed to Rod and Laurel. "I take it that you haven't read too many of your sister's books."

Rod shook his head. "We read some of her short stories when she started writin' in high school, but after our parents died, we kind of drifted apart. You know how it is."

Rusty held up a hand. "Say no more. I'll tell you what. If you want to know exactly what Celeste did for us, you should read her *Sands of Time* series. Four books, all short novels, easy reading. You can blast through one in a night or two. The longest one is about a hundred and seventy-five pages. I have a spare set. It's all yours. That way, you get the whole picture and in Celeste's own words."

"Which one did you read?"

At the Royal Treat for breakfast the following morning, Rod and Laurel placed their orders before delving into a discussion about their sister's novels.

"*Beneath the Surface*," Laurel replied. "It was about Christian Bayard. I wonder if he signed a release form because Celeste didn't even change his name. It had me in tears. After his mother drowned when he was five, Christian was passed around from one family member to the next and some of them were horribly abusive. He ran away when he was fourteen after one of his uncles doused him in gasoline and tried to light him on fire. Christian jumped into a bay up in Maine and swam for miles to get away. The rest of the book is a pretty wild ride until he got to Rehoboth to become a lifeguard and scuba instructor."

"Yeah, well, you should read *The Pressure at this Depth*. It's about Rusty Dickinson. Just like he said at the funeral, the guy had an idyllic life until his wife was shot during a convenience store holdup in Chicago. Then he started drinkin', lost his job, his house, everything. He almost committed suicide before endin' up here in Rehoboth and turnin' his life around. I ain't much of a reader, but that book kept me up all night."

"Can't wait to dive into the next one," Laurel said.

Rod smirked. "I get the feeling they all end with the main characters coming to Rehoboth."

"Still, you have to admit, Celeste turned out to be an amazing writer. She came a long way from her early stuff." After a pause, Laurel continued. "We really should have read her books while she was alive. We should have been more supportive after Mom and Dad died. Instead, we let her down. Did we ever once come to see her after she moved here? She invited us a few times, but it took her death to get us here."

"I know," Rod sighed. "I feel lousy about that, but to be honest, I never knew how to relate to her. Celeste was just *different*. She was always so damn aloof and withdrawn. It always made things awkward. At least we sent birthday and Christmas cards every year."

"That isn't the same."

The waiter brought their food and they ate in silence. Afterward, Rod picked up the check. As they left the Royal Treat, he pointed toward the boardwalk. "Take the scenic route?" Laurel nodded and they started up Wilmington Avenue.

"I just find all of this hard to believe," she said, as they both slipped off their shoes and started down the ramp onto a beach teeming with activity. "I mean, what could make someone as private as Celeste involve herself with all these troubled people? They said she helped them through their problems, but how? Clearly, they inspired her books, but was she just a shoulder to cry on? Did she lend them money? Did she put them up at her house until they got back on their feet?"

"I can't imagine her doing any of that." Rod glanced over at a group of lifeguards gathered near the water, all wearing the red swimsuits of the Rehoboth Beach Patrol. "But I think I see someone who can answer your questions. Ain't that Christian right there? The one who just tossed his bag beside the lifeguard chair?"

Laurel shaded her eyes and followed Rod's gaze to an attractively tanned, and perfectly toned, young man who shucked off his white T-shirt and dropped it into his bag. *If only I were fifteen years younger...* Once he slipped off his sunglasses, she recognized the face. "Yep, that's him."

As they approached, Christian looked up and waved, almost as if he had expected them.

"Hi, again," Laurel began. "Sorry to bother you."

The lifeguard shrugged. "It's no bother. My shift doesn't start for another ten minutes. It's good to see you again. How do you like Rehoboth?"

"Love it so far," Laurel replied, before asking him to elaborate on what he'd said in his eulogy about Celeste.

"Your sister literally wrote my life story," Christian said.

"Same goes for all the others. So what you read in the books is exactly how she helped us."

Laurel started to reply, but Rod cut her off. "Sorry if I'm a little dense. So the only thing Celeste did was write about your lives and that was all you needed to find direction? We were under the impression that maybe she gave you money or a place to stay."

"Not exactly." Christian held up a hand. "If you two are free tonight around seven, we're having a small memorial for your sister at Rusty's house. You're more than welcome to join us. All of your questions will be answered."

They arrived a few minutes late. Rusty offered them several choices of beverage and Christian volunteered to play bartender. As he made his way back toward the kitchen, the others engaged Rod and Laurel in idle conversation about their stay in Rehoboth. Laurel marveled at Virginia Kent's intricate sleeve of tattoos, revealed by her black tank top, while the reunited couple, Dutch Draper and Carla Dodd, once again stood with their arms around each other as if joined at the hip.

Christian returned with their drinks and Rod and Laurel took seats on the sofa.

"So, following up on our conversation on the beach earlier," Christian began. "When I said your sister literally wrote my life story, I meant that your sister *gave* me my life story." He gestured toward the others. "She gave life to all of us, which is why we call ourselves 'The Celestials.'"

Rod and Laurel exchanged puzzled glances.

"Let me explain." Rusty rose from his easy chair and began

pacing the room as he spoke. "Your sister believed that when a writer creates characters with depth and fully developed backgrounds, and all of the flaws and foibles that make one human, those characters come to life in some other world or dimension."

"And we came to life here," Virginia added.

"Here," Laurel repeated, "in … Rehoboth?"

Rod laughed at Laurel's earnest bewilderment. "Okay, we'll play along. So you're sayin' that our sister created all of you simply by writin' you as characters in her books."

Rusty smiled and pointed at Rod. "Give that man a cigar!"

"That's impossible." Laurel shook her head. "Worse, it's insane. Unless you're God, no one can just create people out of nothing! If Celeste imagined all of you into existence, how could you get by without birth certificates or social security cards?"

Rusty held up a hand. "Celeste didn't create us from nothing. She created us from her beautiful and fertile imagination as well as her desperate loneliness. As for the rest, I'll get to that shortly." He stood beside Christian as he continued. "I'm not sure if you had much chance to explore the town, but just up the road, there are intersecting streets named Christian and Bayard." He gestured to the others in turn as he continued. "On the north end of town, we have Virginia Avenue and Kent Street. Over by the bay, Dutch Road and Draper Drive and Carla and Dodd Avenues. As for me, the Rusty Rudder restaurant is on Dickinson Street in Dewey Beach. Celeste was a brilliant storyteller, but she didn't work too hard at naming her characters."

Light laughter went around the room as Rusty took a seat on the sofa beside a noticeably trembling Laurel. She shifted closer to her brother as Rusty looked from her to Rod. "The real reason you fell out of touch with Celeste was that she became angry when you both moved away after your parents died. She felt abandoned and that put a strain on your relationship with her. Isn't that right?"

Rod shifted forward in his seat. Laurel knew he wanted nothing more than to escape, but a strange mélange of curiosity and fear kept her riveted. "Yes. She pleaded with us to stay, but we had lives of our own to—"

"We don't owe these people an explanation." Rod took Laurel's hand and gave it a squeeze. "What happened in our family is none of their business. Let's get out of here." He stood, but Laurel's legs refused to budge.

"I understand how you feel." Rusty glanced over at the others before shifting in his seat. "If you'll just indulge me for another minute." He turned toward the nearest end table and opened a drawer. First, he retrieved a pair of white cotton gloves. After donning them, he reached in again and produced a clear acrylic case containing a paperback book in pristine condition. With a gentle push, Rusty slid aside the top of the case. "Not long after your parents died, Celeste finished her first novel."

As if handling the holiest of relics, Rusty held up the book using both hands. It was titled, *While We're Young.* "Frequently, new authors will write themselves into their stories as the protagonist—under a different name, of course. This is one of those occasions. Celeste used some cheap vanity press to publish this. She sold a few hundred copies at most, but never did a second print run. It's mostly forgotten now." Rusty turned the book over and presented it to Laurel and Rod. "Note the main character's siblings mentioned in the back-cover blurb."

With mounting dread, Laurel leaned forward, but she knew what to expect even before she read the names. "Rodney and … Laurel."

Rod shrugged. "Okay, so Celeste named some characters after us. So what? She did *not* create us. We're flesh and blood human beings!"

"No one is contesting that," Rusty said, "but did you happen to read the 'About the Author' page in any of your sister's books? It mentions that Celeste was one of three children. Would you like to hear her bio from her first novel?"

Rusty turned to the final page and read aloud. "Originally from Bethlehem, Pennsylvania, Celeste Jaggar was the *only* child of two incredibly busy parents. At a very early age, Celeste found companionship in such literary characters as Sherlock Holmes, the Three Musketeers, and Isaac Asimov's Lucky Starr." Rusty lowered the book—and his voice—as he looked from Rod to Laurel. "Celeste's ability to alter her reality didn't manifest until she began writing. As her story-telling skills improved, so too did her power. It wasn't long before she was not only altering her own reality, but that of the world at large."

"But I remember my life," Laurel insisted. "All of it. Wouldn't there be gaps in my memory if I was just a product of Celeste's imagination?"

"What were you doing on this day five years ago?"

Laurel shrugged. "I don't know. Probably working."

"So there are gaps in your memory. Hardly anyone remembers every single day of his or her life. We remember significant conversations, events, achievements, relationships. In other words, fragments—and those were provided to us by Celeste. Now, to answer your earlier question about identification ..."

Rusty lifted his wallet from the coffee table. Opening it, he produced a series of cards and laid them out as he spoke. "Social security, driver's license, medical insurance. Hell, even my library card. All of these things came into existence when we did. Celeste was nothing if not thorough.

"So this brings us back to the two of you. While Celeste was writing her first novel, she still lived in Pennsylvania, but was already spending her summer vacations here in Rehoboth. When you strolled the boardwalk this morning, did you happen to venture to the south end? If so, you might have noticed two streets there, one named Rodney and the other, Laurel. Please understand that we've been waiting a long time to meet you both."

Rod was speechless.

Laurel began to weep.

Rusty grinned. "You were the first Celestials."

Phil Giunta's novels include the paranormal mysteries *Testing the Prisoner, By Your Side,* and *Like Mother, Like Daughters.* His short stories appear in such anthologies as *A Plague of Shadows, Beach Nights,* the *ReDeus* mythology series, and the *Middle of Eternity* speculative fiction series, which he created and edited for Firebringer Press. As a member of the Greater Lehigh Valley Writers Group, Phil also penned stories and essays for *Write Here, Write Now, The Write Connections,* and *Rewriting the Past,* three of the group's annual anthologies.

Phil is currently working on the second draft of a science fiction novel while plotting his triumphant escape from the pressures of corporate America where he has been imprisoned for twenty-five years. Visit Phil's website: www.philgiunta.com.

A DAY AT THE BEACH WITH THE GRAMTHROTTLEMAX FAMILY

BY WELDON BURGE

BernluluGruk GramthrottleMax knew Rehoboth wasn't a nude beach. But he also knew that humans wouldn't know if he was naked or not. They had no clue concerning his genitalia, as his "junk," as the humans say, was safely tucked inside the folds of his upper abdomen.

As soon as he and his family slithered from the ocean onto the beach to get some sun, the humans scattered, screaming, snatching up their towels and children, falling over one another as they rushed toward the boardwalk. They left their umbrellas, boogie boards, beach blankets, and coolers of food and drink, fearing for their lives. At least the two GramthrottleMax kids would have plenty to play with.

The Rehoboth boardwalk fascinated BernluluGruk. He had always wanted to try the saltwater taffy at the Candy Kitchen. He heard the mint sticks were to die for. But, if he tried to climb onto the boardwalk with his massive, sluglike bulk, he surely *would* die.

And Thrasher's french fries! During an earlier visit to the beach, he'd found a box of the fries left behind by fleeing humans. They were delicious—the humans, but especially the fries. He never understood why they were French—but, oh my

God, they smelled so good he really would die for some of them.

His mate, FrizzlegumMash, had for years hounded him to lose weight. He could certainly stand to lose a few hundred pounds. But, weighing in at three tons, he didn't see the sense of it. A bucket of fries wouldn't kill him.

"Where are the kids?" he asked.

"Oh, they've nearly finished eating the lifeguard," FrizzlegumMash said. "They were getting a bit peckish and cranky. So, I told them to run off and get a bite."

The two little guys, FlemrashKrup and SnoopraraNuf, were a rambunctious and ravenous pair. Of course, "little" was open to interpretation. Flem weighed a healthy half ton, and his older brother, Snoop, was now nearly a ton. They grow so fast.

Frizzle, however, thought their offspring were undernourished. BernluluGruk wished she thought *he* was undernourished. You can't eat kelp and plankton forever. This vegan thing was ridiculous. He managed to sneak a harbor seal, sea turtle, or scuba diver when she wasn't looking. (Although the rubber casing of the latter inevitably snarled his mandibles.)

"Bernie, did you remember to bring the suntan lotion?" she asked.

"You know I can't wear that stuff. Slides right off with the rest of the slime."

"Well, don't complain about sunburn later, then. But we do need to slather the kids." She turned. "Flem. Snoop. Get over here!"

BernluluGruk loved Rehoboth Beach. Sure, he and the family often visited Atlantic City at the Jersey shore. The pollution there was delightful, and the occasional corpse floating south from New York City was a special treat (well, if you spit out the bullets). Ocean City, Maryland, and Virginia Beach had been frequent vacation spots as well, and they even traveled as far south as the Outer Banks. But his family preferred Rehoboth Beach. Unfortunately, the denizens of the Delaware beach town were not so fond of the GramthrottleMaxes. Probably that whole eating-of-humans thing.

The family usually had an hour or two on the beach until the humans started pestering them. You'd think humans would be prepared for his family's visits. But, no, it was a new adventure every time.

BernluluGruk reclined in the sand and sighed. A little relaxation time, even if brief, was always welcome. The life of a sea monster could be hectic, especially with a family to feed.

When he first visited Rehoboth Beach with his parents decades before, BernluluGruk assumed the sand would be torture, getting into the creases and crevices of his body, with its blubbery folds and oozing orifices. But the hot beach sand effectively scraped away barnacles—the hotter the sand, the better. And, once back in the water, he found it easy to rinse the sand away. No problem.

His offspring had no reservations about the sand. They rolled and played, tossing sand with abandon. Flinging seashells and seagulls at each other. Making sandcastles and gleefully kicking them down. Eating the occasional human.

FrizzlegumMash, on the other hand, never really enjoyed the beach. But then she had several additional orifices that were not so sand-friendly. He understood.

BernluluGruk knew that, apart from the sand, Frizzlegum-Mash would have liked to lie back and read a book, like many of the beachgoers they had watched from the waves. Maybe something juicy like *Fifty Shades of Grey Whale*. But, of course, publishing was next to impossible back home at the bottom of the Hatteras Abyssal Plain. So, no books. It would be difficult for her to flip through the pages anyway, having no fingers.

BernluluGruk stared at Frizzle for a moment, admiring her elephantine nakedness. He felt lucky to have found her, and even luckier that she had accepted him. Miracles do happen. He never understood why human males got all slobbery over scrawny, stick-thin females wearing tiny string bikinis. Those females were barely snacks—no meat at all. The males seemed to get all excited over two fabric-strapped breasts. Good Lord, why? FrizzlegumMash had eight glorious breasts. What's not to love? And she was the smartest creature on the planet. Certainly smarter than he was.

"Gorgeous," BernluluGruk said. He winked as she turned to him.

"What?" she said. "What? Do you have something in your eye?"

"No. I just wanted you to know how beautiful you are."

"I think you've been in the sun too long. Really."

"Gorgeous," he repeated.

"Bernie, how long do we have to stay here? This sand—"

"Just until the kids get tired. Or the humans decide we've worn out our welcome."

"Well, that may be sooner than you think. The humans are already being forced to leave."

BernluluGruk turned toward the boardwalk. Uniformed men and women were now shepherding people, orchestrating the evacuation. The usual routine, just standard human protocol. The National Guard would arrive soon. He and his family still had time to enjoy the beach before the firepower showed up.

He and Frizzle loved the mayhem that typically ensued— and the accompanying feast. BernluluGruk liked to think of it as a buffet on the beach. But he knew the little ones couldn't tolerate the explosions and thunderous noise for long. The screams from the humans, no problem. But the grenades and rocket-launchers, not so much.

"Should we start packing?" FrizzlegumMash asked.

"Nah. I think we have time. Let the kids play a little longer. Besides, I'm quite comfortable here. The sun is wonderful. The barnacles are silently screaming. And I can already feel the vitamin D building in my body fat."

"That's nice, dear." She turned to the kids playing in the sand. "FlemrashKrup GramthrottleMax! Stop gnawing on that seagull. You'll get feathers in your mandibles."

"Listen to your mother," said BernluluGruk. "We'll have enough to eat shortly. Wouldn't you much prefer a tasty human over that measly seagull?"

"Bernie! Stop it," FrizzlegumMash said, nudging him with a flipper. "You're going to spoil them."

"Aw, Mom," Flem said. He tossed the maimed seagull aside.

BernluluGruk yawned, much like most sea monsters do. The yawn sounded simultaneously like an angry pelican and a flatulent walrus. Only sea monster vocal chords can accomplish this.

"Let me know when the soldier boys get here," he said, closing his eyes.

BernluluGruk must have dozed off. How long? Maybe an hour. Maybe only minutes.

FrizzlegumMash leaned into him. "Do you hear that?"

BernluluGruk heard them before he saw them. Fighter jets, probably scrambled from the Dover Air Force Base. No National Guard this time. Just all-out warfare. And, unfortunately, no easy meals.

The jets would arrive in seconds.

"Time to go, Frizzle," he said. "Talk about taking the fun out of it. Jets? Really? Not the National Guard? Where's the fun in that?"

There were two jets screaming toward them from the north. At that moment, BernluluGruk wished he'd been Godzilla, able to swat the planes from the sky. (Of course, Godzilla was an irritable bastard, and BernluluGruk usually stayed away from him at dinner parties. That breath!)

"Flem. Snoop," BernluluGruk said, heaving himself from the sand. "We need to leave now."

"Aww, Dad," they whined in unison.

"Can't we stay a little longer?" Snoop asked.

"We can come back another time. Perhaps next week, if the weather is nice. But, right now, we need to gather our things and head to the water."

"What things?" FrizzlegumMash asked. "We're naked."

"I mean any things the kids want to take with them. Maybe a seagull or two. Your sunscreen. What's left of that lifeguard. Just hurry."

Even though the jets were still just two dots in the sky,

BernluluGruk saw the flashes beneath them and knew missiles were on the way. He'd never dealt with missiles before, but he was always up for a new challenge.

BernluluGruk couldn't believe how quickly the missiles arrived. The first missile plunged into his gelatinous left side. He plucked it from his body with a tentacle and hurled it into the ocean, where it exploded in a mushroom of seawater. The wound did hurt a bit—like a bubble of gas in his intestine, something difficult to pass but of no real concern.

He flipped the second missile into the water with his back fin. Another explosion of seawater. The third, he disposed of with a whip-like tentacle. The fourth, he slapped easily aside, and it exploded in the sand.

He was getting the hang of it.

Two F-15 jets zoomed overhead. BernluluGruk knew they would circle back for another attack.

"Get the kids into the water, Friz. As deeply and as quickly as you can. I'm their largest target, so they'll pay no mind to you and the kids—at least for now. Once you're safe, I'll follow."

FrizzlegumMash prodded Flem and Snoop toward the surf. But, apparently reluctant to leave, they moved with something less than urgency, flopping more than slithering to the water. Frizzle prodded more.

"Hurry!" BernluluGruk said. "They're returning. Get into the water!"

The jets had turned and now approached again. But BernluluGruk saw no flashes of missiles this time. How many missiles did the typical fighter jet carry? He had no idea. Maybe they planned a strafing run this time, which would make more sense. Perhaps they didn't want to destroy the beach—just destroy him.

The jets zoomed toward him. He didn't budge, giving the pilots a massive, perfect target. He glanced over at his family. They had reached the surf and would soon find safety in the ocean.

And then the jets passed overhead. They did not attack him, for whatever reason. Maybe they'd watched him swat the earlier missiles aside and determined that another air strike would be fruitless.

He assumed that meant the armed forces would arrive soon. That was always fun, but he'd had enough sun and fun for the day. The family was already in the water, waiting for him.

He sighed, shrugged his three shoulders, and moved toward the surf.

The GramthrottleMax family would return to Rehoboth Beach again before the summer was over. Perhaps several times.

He really was hankering for some Thrasher's fries.

Weldon Burge, a native of Delaware, is a full-time editor, freelance writer, and publisher. His fiction has appeared in many publications, including various magazines and anthologies (*The Best of the Horror Society 2013, Pellucid Lunacy: An Anthology of Psychological Horror, Ghosts and Demons*, just to name a few). His stories have also been adapted for podcast presentation by Drabblecast. Weldon is a frequent writer for *Suspense Magazine*, often writing author interviews. Starting in 2012, he and his wife, Cindy, founded Smart Rhino Publications (www.smartrhino.com), an indie publishing company focusing primarily on horror and suspense/thriller books.

MYSTERY OF THE MISSING GIRL SLEUTH

BY BARBARA NORTON

She walked into his office like she owned it. Tight suit. Fashionable beret and ladylike high-heeled shoes. Curves that could turn any sucker's head. Great gams, encased in silk stockings, even in the ninety-degree heat. A real class act. At least that's what he thought at first. Later, his opinion changed.

"The paint on your sign is peeling," she said. "Is this 22222-A Rehoboth Avenue, the business establishment of a Mr. Nathan (The Nose) McGee, private investigator?" She had a surprisingly squeaky, New Jersey-tinged voice that grated on the ear like nails on a blackboard. To be honest, the pipes didn't exactly match the rest of the package.

"You're lookin' at him, sweetheart. Sorry about the sign. It's tough to keep paint looking good here at the beach. Please, have a seat," he said, indicating a wicker chair he'd rescued from his grandma's back porch.

This broad can't be more than sixteen or seventeen years old. Jailbait. What's she doing here? He rushed to raise the shades and open the door so anyone passing could see there was no hanky-panky going on.

"Let me turn the fan toward you." He may have been a middle-aged, pot-bellied ex-cop with only an eighth-grade education, but he could be a gentleman. The little electric fan that blew hot air from the screened window behind his desk did little to relieve the stifling heat and humidity, and it had the negative effect of messing up the little lady's hair.

"Hey, moron, turn that thing away from me."

"Oh, sure." So much for gentlemanly charm. Sensing the meeting wasn't going well, he started to ask her why she was in his office, but then a light bulb of recognition flashed in his noggin. "Say, I know you. Ain't you that Nancy Drew? I seen your picture on my kid's book. She tells me about all them mysteries you solve. Well, I'll be damned … I mean darned. Nancy Drew, a celebrity, right here in little old Rehoboth Beach, Delaware."

"Don't believe everything you read, pops. We work for the same syndicate, her and me, and we may look a little alike, but we are two very different characters. My name is Stella Strong. I guess you could say The Boss created me as a kind of insurance policy in case the public wanted two girl sleuths, not one. Two, like in those other kid series—the Bobbsey Twins and the Hardy Boys."

"Yeah, my son loves them. Wait a minute. Did you say you work for the Syndicate?" McGee started to sweat bullets, and it wasn't just the heat. "I learned a long time ago not to mess with the Syndicate."

"Not the mob, moron, it's a literary syndicate. You know, newspapers, books, that sort of thing. Anyway, here's my problem. Everybody loves Nancy Drew and she's a big hit. But here's the catch. It's in *my* contract (and my lawyer says it's iron-tight) that if anything happens to Miss Goody Two-Shoes and she can't continue the series, I'm stuck pretending to be her. God knows how long that series could run. They've pumped out ten books just since 1930."

"So?"

"Please, I've no one else to turn to. You've got to help me. If I have to stay seventeen forever, and be sweet, and put up with Ned Nickerson, her all-American bore of a boyfriend, I just don't know what I'll do. She took a lace handkerchief from her clutch purse and pretended to bawl into it.

"Quit it, doll. You must think I'm a real sap. I can't do nothing about a contract, anyways. I investigate cheatin' husbands, murders, missing persons … that sort of thing."

She sat up straight. "Missing persons. Bingo! That's why I'm here, detective. Nancy Drew has gone missing." She peeked over her hanky. "I tried to call her author, Carolyn Keene, to see if she knows what happens next, but for some reason she never answers her phone."

"How do you know she's missing?"

"I don't know. It's like a twin thing. Whenever she's in trouble, I just know."

"Well, I ain't never pursued a fictional character before, but if it pays, I'm in. My fee is ten bucks a day and I don't take any of that funny money like they sell in the dime store. But first I need answers to a few questions. Where was she last seen, how long has she been missing, and did she leave any clues about what might have happened to her?"

"Just this," Stella said, as she pulled a piece of paper out of her clutch and began unfolding it. "She's a lousy artist, but I think this stick drawing is a dog, or maybe a horse, standing in front of a big wagon wheel. It makes no sense. I ripped it out of the sketch pad she left sitting on her beach blanket. She must have taken the pencil with her, because I looked around and it wasn't there. It couldn't have happened very long ago. I came as soon as I had that bad feeling I told you about."

"Didn't anyone see her leave the beach?"

"The lifeguard said he was busy lookin' toward the ocean, but he did notice she was wearing a perky yellow sundress over her bathing suit when she arrived with her blanket and sketch book. The boy that rents chairs and umbrellas said he saw a man with a straw hat and fancy suit come up to her. The guy pulled her arm as they left the beach. He had his hat pulled down low, so the kid couldn't see the guy's face."

"Didn't the kid call the cops?" McGee asked.

"Nah, he just thought it was her father. He did say the guy looked angry, like maybe he didn't like her sittin' there showing her ankles and bare feet for all the world to see. But it couldn't have been him, because I called their house and the maid said Mr. Drew's in court today."

McGee's daughter had told him that Nancy's father was a criminal defense attorney, so that made sense. "Where was she sitting?"

"Not far from that taffy place with the big 'Dolles' sign."

"Hmmm. Show me where, so I can check it out myself." McGee reached for his hat and the garish plaid summer suit jacket hanging on a hook near the door. "We could walk it, but let's take my Plymouth. It's parked out back, behind the office. Used to be my squad car before I retired from the force. She's got some miles on her, but still runs like new."

He gave Stella his hand as she stepped up onto the running

board and held the door while she got in. "Hold onto your hat, dearie," he said, as he pulled out onto Rehoboth Avenue. "She sputters a little 'till she gets up to speed."

They headed away from the ocean, until a break in the sand and grass median allowed them to make a U-turn back toward the beach.

"Look! I didn't see that before." Stella pointed to a stylish powder-blue roadster, parked on a side street a block away from the boards. "That's Nancy's car, and—surprise, surprise—Mr. Useless All-American Ned Nickerson is in it, napping in the back seat. I'll bet he doesn't even know she's missing." They pulled up alongside the car.

"Ned, wake up," Stella yelled. "Have you seen Nancy?"

The groggy high school football star sat up and yawned. He wore a black tank top that showed off his muscular shoulders and arms, and fashionable belted swim trunks that emphasized his trim waist.

"Huh? Oh, hi, Nancy. I must have dozed off. Say, why are you wearing that? I thought we were going bathing in the ocean?" He yawned. "Or did we already do that?"

"You're such a numbskull," Stella said, sighing angrily. "I'm Stella, Stella Strong, you empty-headed barbell. Nancy has red hair with blonde highlights, and I have blonde hair with red highlights. Anyone can tell the difference. We're looking for Nancy. Has she come back to the car?"

"Oh, yeah. Hi, Stella." Ned scratched his head. "Not unless she came by while I was dozing. Should we look for her or something?"

"No. You stay here in case Nancy comes back," Stella said.

"Come look for us on the beach or boardwalk if that happens."

McGee pulled the Plymouth into a neighboring cottage's driveway, backed out, and headed back to the Avenue, parking a few spaces from the boards. Stella carried her shoes as they hurried down the steps, hotfooted it across the burning white sand, and found the empty blanket.

"Oh, I know," Stella cried, picking up the sketch book. "I should have noticed that right away. She was facing the boards when she was sketching, not the ocean. This drawing must be one of the ponies at the Funland carousel. And that wheel thing behind it must be the Ferris wheel." She placed a manicured red fingertip on her cheek and blinked her baby blues. "I wonder if she was giving us a clue."

"Whoa, whoa, whoa, sweet cheeks. Hold on there," McGee said. "I beg to inform you that this is 1935 and there is no Ferris wheel or Funland in Rehoboth Beach. Not to say there won't be someday," he added.

She gave him a sideways glance. "This is fiction—you know, *make-believe*. Suspend disbelief, moron. We need there to be a Ferris wheel to advance the plot and come up with a jaw-dropping climax."

"Oh, well, okay. It's your story," he said, tipping his hat. "We'll play it your way. Let's go."

But before they could step off the blanket, the chair boy came running up to Stella and tugged on her arm. "Hey, lady," he said. "You still looking for that dame in the yellow sundress?"

"Yes. Have you seen her?"

The boy pointed toward the Ferris wheel and said, "I think that's her up there at the top, hanging over the side of the car."

"Aw, jeez," McGee said. The wheel that had to be thirty feet tall wasn't going around, but the little red car at the top was swaying wildly.

"Help!" Nancy screamed, as a man struggled to throw her over the side. The guard bar was open and dangled off to one side. Nancy was clinging to the front rim of the car, trying to brace herself with her feet against the metal. If the evil man succeeded, she would surely meet her death on the boards below.

McGee couldn't tell which broad was screaming louder, the victim atop the Ferris wheel or Miss Stella Strong, who was sprinting down the boards ahead of him at Olympic-runner speed.

"No! No! You're not going to die today, Nancy Drew! Hold on. I'm coming!" Stella raced through the small crowd that had gathered to watch what was happening, shoved the young Ferris wheel operator aside, and pushed the control forward to get the wheel moving again. Nothing happened.

"It's stuck, lady!" the operator yelled. "That man up there must have jammed something into it, so it would stop when his car reached the top. He was rude and chased away all my other customers. It's just those two people stuck at the top. I've been trying to—"

"Try harder," Stella demanded. "Listen, see, this is important … a matter of life or death. I need you to help me push the lever. When I count to three, give it everything you've got. One, two …" At three, they shoved the lever forward with all their might. The gears clanked into place, and the tinny circus music that was timed to the turning of the giant wheel began blaring. The Ferris wheel's empty cars rocked, and onlookers gasped as the octopus-like iron and steel structure shivered from the strain.

The jerking of the start-up threw the villain backward, causing him to momentarily lose his grip on Nancy and fall into the bench seat. That gave the intrepid girl detective a moment to catch her breath, but only a moment, because he was determined to kill the girl sleuth, and when he came back behind her it was with both his hands wrapped around her pretty little neck. It was a race against time. Which would come first? The car reaching the bottom, or the life oozing out of Nancy Drew?

Never one to be a quitter, even when the chips were down, Nancy reached into the pocket of her sundress and withdrew the sharpened No. 2 pencil she had used while she was sketching. With her almost-last breath, she reached back over her right shoulder and drove the pencil into the man's cheek. Now he was screaming in pain, but thanks to the teenaged detective's grit and ingenuity, she would live to solve many more mysteries, and the villain would be going to jail.

"Thank Gawd, Thank Gawd," Stella yelled, as she ran to McGee, who had taken out his gun and was holding it on the bad guy as the car made its way down. She jumped up and down with excitement. "Now I don't have to pretend to be Nancy Drew." She gave him a big hug and kissed him on the cheek.

"Hey, hey. Easy there, sweetheart. We don't want this guy to get away. Somebody must have called the station. I hear the sirens coming up the Avenue. You know, you owe me ten bucks for the day."

"Sure, sure, gladly," she said, reaching into her bra to take out the cash.

He tried not to look.

Ned Nickerson strolled up, just in time to help Nancy out of the ride's car. He didn't seem to notice that the man seated next to her had a pencil jammed into his face. "Aw, you should have come and gotten me," he scolded. "I love it when we ride the Ferris wheel."

She smiled. "Why don't you go get the roadster," she suggested. "I don't think I'm really up for a swim." He jogged happily down the boardwalk toward the side street where the car waited.

"Say," McGee said to Nancy. "I'm interested. Do you know who that guy was who was trying to rub you out?"

"Yes. I'm pretty sure I've seen him before. He works for my publisher's rival. They've been trying to get the syndicate to dump my current publisher and sign with them. Don't worry. I've got it under control. You can learn more about it in my next episode, "Mystery of the Missing Manuscript.""

"I bet my kid will love that one," McGee said with a wink.

AUTHOR'S NOTE

Who Really Wrote the Nancy Drew Novels?

Ahhh … therein lies the real mystery of Nancy Drew. Although the Stratemeyer Syndicate worked hard to make it appear that author Carolyn Keene was a real person, in fact, she was not. Edward Stratemeyer, founder of the syndicate and author of the very popular Bobbsey Twins and Hardy Boys series, created the concept of girl sleuth Nancy Drew in 1929. In his proposal for the series, her name was Stella Strong. Stratemeyer, and later, his daughter Harriet Stratemeyer Adams, supplied ghostwriters with detailed plot outlines and character guidelines. Harriet and a journalist named Mildred Wirth Benson wrote most of the series. It ended in 2003 and, although Nancy evolved with the times (particularly her fashion), she forever remained a teenager who loved to solve mysteries.

To learn more, read Melanie Rehak's *Girl Sleuth, Nancy Drew and the Women Who Created Her* (Dutton Publishing, 2005).

Like generations of teenage girls, Barbara Norton grew up devouring Nancy Drew mysteries. Still an avid reader and a fan of other mystery series writers like Lisa Scottoline and Linda Fairstein, Barbara is currently writing the second in her White House Correspondent Jillian Rain mystery/thrillers, titled *Blue Butterfly*. The first was *Breaking News*. She is also author of *The Jewels*, an historical fiction thriller. Follow her at www.BarbNorton.com.

OPERATION STEAMED

I hadn't eaten a blue crab in over twenty years, hadn't set foot on the Eastern Shore in a quarter century. Maybe longer. In fact, as far as I was concerned, if I never saw another crab for the rest of my life, well, that'd be just fine with me. It didn't even dawn on me when I accepted the invitation to a cookout at my friend's house over Memorial Day weekend that the entire engagement would be just a big ole Maryland crab feast.

The memories flooded back as soon as I got out of my car—the smell of Old Bay wafting on the breeze, the sight of foldout tables covered in brown butcher paper, mounds of orange crabs steaming in the center of each one.

It was the summer of 1986, and I was a college student living and working in Ocean City, Maryland. The Cold War was still on, and tensions were high between the United States and the Soviet Union, although the only thing cold I paid any attention to was the cheap cans of domestic I drank with my roommates every night. I only know what happened because I was there. And when it was all over, I knew too much. What I'm about to relate may seem outlandish; preposterous, even. It is. And it's all true.

Dr. Gordon told me the idea began quite by accident one

night when he—a research scientist who worked at Aberdeen Proving Grounds—was at home, up late, watching an old black-and-white movie. Giant mutated ants were roaming the lands of New Mexico. Fallout from atomic tests in Alamogordo had changed them into massive man-eating monsters.

The Chernobyl disaster had just taken place and the United States was not getting much information out of the Soviet Union. There were some who thought that the Soviets were trying to exploit the meltdown for their own diabolical purposes—closing down the area and conducting tests on how radiation might change the flora and fauna, with visions of military use.

Gordon had watched the ants wreak havoc and couldn't help but think of what the Reds might be up to. He returned to the lab the following day with a brilliant idea: what if it were possible to alter the genetic makeup of a smaller creature, like an ant, so that it could be used militarily? Imagine transporting these creatures to the battlefield in their natural state—small, concealable, easy to carry—and then transforming them into giant killing machines on enemy ground.

And what better area to conduct these tests? The proving grounds' neighbor, Edgewood Arsenal, had long been a site for testing chemical weapons. From the 1940s through the Vietnam War, Edgewood conducted tests on animals (including humans in some cases) using sarin, nerve gas, and even LSD. Rumors were that in the early years some of these programs were led by former Nazi scientists, who were brought covertly to the United States, in what was known as Operation Paperclip.

Gordon's superiors at Aberdeen were all for testing the idea that small creatures could be genetically altered to become weapons. Stupendous! Revolutionary!

They put Gordon in touch with Dr. Sellers (who turned out to be a former Nazi researcher, now an American scientist) and the two began collaborating on this new possibility at once.

Although an old man by now, Sellers felt reborn with this new directive. The scientific method was put to good use again and again, and progress seemed to come quickly. Gordon had never met a more brilliant mind—twisted, yes, but brilliant, nonetheless. Gordon was eager to learn all he could from this man. The two worked tirelessly, almost around the clock.

Ants, wasps, spiders, scorpions. All incubated safely away from the public, their bodies flowing with toxic chemicals, every piece of each creature prodded and poked, measured and recorded.

"What about aquatics? A naval creature, something that could attack from water and move onto to dry land, before returning safely back to the sea? The creatures could be released off the coast, even dropped from the air, to swim to land and attack." Sellers smiled wickedly.

Dr. Gordon picked up where Sellers left off. "A dual assault. Land and naval attacks, coordinated simultaneously. Brilliant."

Sellers sighed. "We just need a test subject."

Gordon looked out the window, the Chesapeake Bay barely visible in the distance. "What about a crab?"

The first attack happened just after dawn at the Perdue

plant in Salisbury, Maryland. A night security guard had been ripped to shreds and over six hundred pounds of raw chicken had been stolen. A massive hole was left in the side of the building, thought to have come from some type of blast, although no explosive residue was ever found. A second watchman was taken to Peninsula General Hospital for observation, babbling incoherently. "The crab! The crab!"

I'd been a bad boy the night before, couldn't even remember her name. Just before dawn I snuck out of her rathole Ocean City apartment somewhere on Robin Drive, and in my bleary drunken state wandered the wrong way, ending up at a dead end overlooking Assawoman Bay. The air was still; humidity hung like an unwelcome wool blanket, the blue hour casting everything in black silhouette against an empty August sky. Assawoman was a sheet of glass and as I retched vomit into still water, the bay rippled in outward rings, big chunks of last night's pizza floating lazily on the surface. My head throbbed with pain.

I slumped in the sandy soil, a small stream of bile running down my chin, and hung my head in defeat before the day had even begun.

Splashing sounds startled me back to life. As I turned, and I'll never forget this 'til the day I die, I saw a massive black shadow moving at the edge of the water. Peering over for a closer look, I could see jaws feeding on my leftovers, two long antennae like black ropes waving back and forth, and two black eyes shining like obsidian in the moonlight. The reality didn't fully register until a massive claw rose from the water like some mythological creature from Homer, its sights set on me, lying passive and pickled in the predawn.

The claw opened and the jaws of the monstrous crustacean moved excitedly, a loud clicking sound emanating from somewhere inside the belly of the beast. I jumped up and ran as fast as my wobbly legs would carry me, crossing Coastal Highway without bothering to look for traffic.

The shaking had stopped by the time the bus arrived and I rode in horrified silence back to the high-rises of north Ocean City, unsure what to do with my unwanted knowledge.

I didn't have to think long.

The third attack, the one that changed everything, never officially happened. Even to this day, the government refuses to attribute the incident to anything other than a workplace accident. A ride malfunction. Mass hysteria.

Those who were there know better. Those who were there know the truth.

The time between the Perdue incident and my experience was just over two days. The third attack occurred just under nine hours later. Exhausted and confused from the morning's trauma, I had returned to our shabby rental on Jamestown Road for some much-needed rest. By noon I was feeling somewhat recharged, lounging on the musty sofa, a Styrofoam container of chicken wings on my lap.

"Look what I got."

I glanced up at one of my roommates, Bill, who was decked out in flowered surf trunks, a beach towel wrapped around his neck. He was holding something in his hand.

"What's that?"

Bill's gaze shifted over to the food in the container. He came over, stuffed an entire chicken wing in his mouth and mumbled, "Jolly Roger—*Jarry Rar-Rar.*" Then he tossed the bone back. "All-day passes to the water park. Let's go."

I should have stayed in bed. I should have realized before I agreed to go, that Jolly Roger was downtown, and actually bordered Robin Drive. I should have …

The water park was packed. I've never understood why so many tourists, who paid so much money to come to the beach, would drop even more cash on a beautiful summer's day playing on a waterslide when they could ride the ocean waves for free. But clearly Jolly Roger was doing something right. And, truth be told, the waterslide was pretty kick-ass.

We didn't notice anything unusual at first. It was, after all, an amusement park. Lots of action—little kids screaming, water splashing, go-karts flying around, their lawn mower engines rumbling loudly. We didn't notice anything until we were at the top of the waterslide awaiting our turn to drop. The view from that height is pretty spectacular, and as I stood in front of Bill, next in line to go, I could clearly see the complex on Robin Drive where I'd spent the previous night, the bay looking blue and serene from that far away. It was Bill who pointed it out to me. The swirling cloud of deep red in the wave pool below us.

Watching humans panic in a large crowd is almost humorous. The blood cloud floated lazily in the pool, swirling with currents created by flailing arms and kicking legs, small white splashes erupting from the turquoise-blue water. It would have made a great piece of modern art. And then the running began. People scattered in all directions, some rushing toward Coastal Highway, others toward the parking lot. Parents frantically searched for their children. We watched all of this from above, seemingly detached from the horrific events taking place below.

The lifeguard sitting on his stool next to me watched disinterestedly, his Walkman cranking hair metal in his ears.

He nodded at me. "Next."

As I stepped toward the drop, a massive claw came from nowhere and snatched the unsuspecting guard from his perch, the Walkman dropping to the wooden planks where his feet had rested not two seconds before. People screamed, some pushing forward, others trying to run back down the steps they had just climbed. I grabbed Bill and we jumped onto the waterslide, a mass of tourists following suit, and we all came tumbling down in one endless line of freaked-out humanity. The small pool could not contain us all and a pile of bodies began to grow as more and more people rode the waterslide down. Bill and I managed to swim beneath the heap of elbows and knees, making our way to the edge of the pool.

That was when I heard a loud clicking from above.

The giant crab was hanging from the wooden framework of the waterslide, antennae waving wildly, like flags in an ocean breeze, its hideous jaws moving back and forth excitedly. A portion of an arm hung from its mouth. The monster's claw snapped wildly at the waterslide, snatched a small child, and began to climb the rickety support columns. The old wooden beams creaked in protest and the entire waterslide began to slowly sway. I grabbed Bill and we began to make our way out through the miniature golf course. The creaking grew louder, from a whisper to a scream, and the entire structure fell to the ground like tinker toys pushed over by a bully.

The crab landed directly in front of us.

I grabbed a mini-golf club and tossed another one to Bill, the two of us striking at the brute with the heads of our putters. We managed to inflict enough damage that the crab dropped the crying child and turned its attention toward us, razor-sharp claws snapping dangerously close. A few other brave souls followed suit, and collectively we were able to beat the leviathan back until, at last, it retreated into the waters of Assawoman Bay.

That night the entire town of Ocean City was placed under a mandatory curfew from sunset to sunrise. Local, state, and federal law enforcement vehicles patrolled the streets. Military vehicles passed up and down Coastal Highway. The sound of helicopter rotor blades beating against the summer sky echoed off the faces of the high-rise towers all night long like the pounding of a pulsing heart. Tourists and residents were told that the town was on lockdown while authorities pursued an escaped prisoner from the Sussex Correctional Institution in Georgetown, Delaware.

Bill and I knew different.

The following morning, heavy clouds hung low over the barrier islands of the Eastern Shore. Rain squalls passed through all day, and although the curfew was not in effect once it was light, most people didn't seem to have the energy to venture outside. There was a story on the local news about family pets that had gone missing overnight. Most of the animals lived in Ocean Pines, houses on, or close to, Assawoman Bay. The boys on Jamestown Road spent the afternoon drinking beer, Bill and I trying to forget what had happened just twenty-four hours earlier.

At seven thirty that evening the alarm sirens rang once, reminding everyone that the curfew would begin in thirty minutes. When the final siren finished wailing its sad song at eight o'clock, I rose from our kitchen table without a sound and exited the apartment. My roommates sat slack-jawed, saying nothing, as I wandered out into the approaching darkness.

At the end of Jamestown, where it intersects Coastal Highway, I turned right and began walking down the center of the road, heading south. A tank stopped me in front of the Gold Coast Mall, its round muzzle staring me in the face like some strange Cyclops eye.

Soldiers shoved me to the pavement, tossed me into the back of a Humvee, and drove me two blocks up the road to a makeshift headquarters located in the basement of the Carousel Hotel. After some babbling on my part about crabs, conspiracies, and cover-ups, they led me to a small room and told me to take a seat on a pile of cardboard boxes. Liquor storage. Before I could partake of a bottle, two men entered the room, followed by two armed guards.

Dr. Gordon and Dr. Sellers were more than a little curious about what I had seen—what I knew or thought I knew about the *specimen*.

"Mass hysteria." Sellers smiled when he said this, his German-influenced English biting the very air around him. He rolled his hand nonchalantly, "Ahh, you see a mass hysteria caused by a contagion in the pool, *en zee pool water.* Very easy to explain away." His eyes narrowed. "But you, you my friend, are not so easy to explain away, are you?"

I leaned back in my makeshift chair, grabbed a bottle of Absolut, cracked the seal, and drank a long swig. "Well, doctors, if you're so smart then why are we even having this conversation? I mean, my guess is that you two are somehow responsible for creating this mess, or you wouldn't be here, right? But hey, you don't need to hear my plan on how to capture this crab—I mean—this *specimen.*"

Gordon looked from me to Sellers, the two men passing this idea between them. Finally, Sellers nodded his consent. Gordon spoke, "Well then, let's hear it."

Sellers and Gordon returned to their lab at once, still uncertain about the outcome of their latest experiment. Could something dead—freshly killed, but dead—be altered genetically in the same way? Could a heart or a liver, detached from its host, but still filled with fresh blood, grow in size? What about chicken parts?

The answer came on the third attempt in the form of a chicken neck the size of a full-grown man. The doctors packed the bait in ice, loaded it into the back of an LMTV military transport, and drove the three hours from Aberdeen to Ocean City, rolling into town beneath an umbrella of sunset clouds washing the sky in golden twilight. They parked the vehicle behind the Rose's on 94th Street.

A curfew siren wailed.

I stood alongside Sellers and Gordon as the men finished their prep work on the 94th Street water tower.

Gordon shook his head and laughed, "This might just be crazy enough to work."

As night settled over the town, a sudden power outage plunged Ocean City into darkness. The doctors attached the chicken neck to a long cable as a Chinook helicopter hovered over the water tower, lifting the top half off like the lid being removed from a Weber kettle grill. The cabled chicken neck was remotely winched up the side of the water tower, facing out toward Devil Island, a small wildlife area behind the mall.

"What now?" Sellers asked. *Vut now?*

"Now, fellas," I said. "Now, we wait."

We didn't hear the clicking noise until almost sunrise. The crab must have come out of one of the canals a little farther south, probably attracted by the nasty smell of rotting chicken neck wafting in the breeze. The beast followed Rusty Anchor Road to where it intersects 94th Street, its massive jaws clicking ferociously.

An armed soldier drew his gun to fire, but the crab's claw snatched him and tossed him aside, his weapon discharging wildly.

"Cease fire! Cease fire!" Sellers screamed.

Everyone took a step backward except Dr. Sellers, who walked toward the creature. He turned, his eyes glowing, a hideous smile spreading across his haggard face. The old man's hands trembled with excitement. "Beautiful. Just beautiful. It is—"

And before he could complete the sentence, the monster

had him in his claw, antennae waving wildly.

Sellers let out a blood-curdling scream as the crustacean popped him in its mouth, its mighty jaws crushing the man to death. The crab then turned its attention to the giant chicken neck dangling from the blue water tower. As it latched onto the bait, feeding on raw flesh, the winch slowly pulled the beast up.

The crab feasted, unawares, as it was hoisted up the side of the water tower and into the makeshift steamer. The Chinook hovered over Assawoman, the top half of the tower hanging from cables. A smaller helicopter flew above the crab, dropping a half ton of Old Bay seasoning on top of the crustacean.

The mutant reared up, both claws snapping wildly at the rotorcraft, almost grabbing hold of one of the landing skids. As the smaller aircraft lifted safely away, the Chinook moved in and dropped the top half of the water tower onto its base.

Enormous propane tanks connected to gas lines that ran up through the interior of the tower were turned on and a makeshift igniter supplied the spark. A waterproofed heating element cranked to life and the water slowly began to boil. The monster, now trapped, beat against the inside of its cage, a hollow ringing sound reverberating for blocks.

I swear I saw the structure sway back-and-forth a few times before settling quietly in place.

As the sun rose, beams of glory illuminating a new day, people awoke to the smell of steamed crabs in Ocean City, Maryland.

The breaking news that morning was that the fugitive had been captured overnight and was now safely back in solitary confinement at the Sussex Correctional Facility.

The curfew had been lifted.

And as a special way of showing their appreciation to every-one inconvenienced by this unfortunate situation, the Town of Ocean City held a free crab feast on the beach next to the inlet. No picking necessary—the town had already taken care of that. Just mounds and mounds of steaming crabmeat, waiting to be consumed.

A few days later an article appeared in the *Beachcomber* newspaper detailing an investigation by a local reporter. She had interviewed witnesses who said they clearly saw what looked like a giant crab at the Jolly Roger Amusement Park. Another person came forward to tell a similar tale—only the location was farther uptown, near the Rose's department store.

Just before Labor Day weekend, as I was walking up James-town Road on my way to check the waves, a black sedan pulled alongside. The blacked-out rear window rolled down and Dr. Gordon poked his head out. "A word, please."

I leaned in and saw that Gordon was seated next to a man in military dress, a collection of colorful awards proudly pinned to his mighty chest. His head was shaved nearly bald. Gordon gestured toward the man, "Uhh, this is General—"

The general cut him off before I was able to hear even one syllable of his name. "Son, as you know this little situation is a bit delicate. Without going into any detail, let's just say it would be best for everyone—especially yourself," he pointed an index finger thick as a big toe at my face, "to keep a lid on what you know, or *think* you know."

I wanted out of there. "You got it."

"Good." General stared straight ahead in silence for ten seconds. "Because, son, if any specifics were to get out to the press, well …" He gave me the death stare. "Well, son, accidents happen."

Before I could reply, the blacked-out window rolled back up and the black sedan drove out to Coastal Highway and disappeared.

Back in my dorm room in October of that fall semester of 1986, I was flipping through channels after dinner and saw something interesting pop up. President Reagan and Mikhail Gorbachev were meeting in Reykjavik to discuss the dismantling of all nuclear weapons on the planet. In one of the photographs posted on the screen, standing behind the two leaders, Dr. Gordon and a grim-faced general were clearly visible. One year later, the United States and the Soviet Union signed the INF Treaty, eliminating an entire class of nuclear weapons. It was the beginning of the end of the Cold War.

Did the Soviets know something about what Sellers and Gordon had been up to? Did it scare them enough to agree to such a treaty? The Cold War ended just three years later. The once mighty Soviet Union would cease to exist by the end of 1991. Did Operation Steamed have anything to do with it or am I just grasping at straws?

I take a reluctant seat at the table, a large crab staring up at me. My friend smiles. "Bushel of the jumbos. Ain't they the biggest crabs you've ever seen?"

David Strauss grew up visiting the beach, spending his summers in Clearwater Beach, Florida, and Ocean City, Maryland. He spent his college years living and working in Ocean City, where he delivered pizzas on his bicycle. David has had poetry and/or short stories published in *Damozel, Self X-Press,* and *Dirt Rag* magazines, and in *The Boardwalk, Beach Nights,* and *Beach Life.* He has also published two novels, *Dangerous Shorebreak* and *Structurally Deficient,* through CreateSpace. He teaches US History until he can retire to the beach.

NIGHT FLYER

BY CHRIS JACOBSEN

The Henlopen Hotel, on the boards in Rehoboth, was full to capacity. The bellhop stepped lively and stowed the suitcase inside the guest's room. He gave a nod of thanks for the coin tossed his way. Exiting the room, he winced at his reflection; he could double as an organ-grinder's monkey. Now, the khaki "Class B" army uniforms, with neatly creased caps, brass slide-buckle belts, and low quarter brown shoes; that was a uniform! Soldiers received respectful nods from the men, coy looks of approval from the ladies.

Fort Miles boasted two thousand soldiers. It loomed over the Delaware Bay, to protect the Delaware River and the oil refineries up in Philadelphia. Observation towers allowed for triangulation of German war ships. The naval minefield threatened mincemeat for any stealthy U-boats.

Weekends couldn't come fast enough for the girls in town. They would get dolled up and head to the taverns where GIs went to throw down their drink. A favorite was the Bottle & Cork Taproom, with its sawdust floor, lively music, and hearty food. Some girls went for dancing, some for free drinks, and others to find love. But none realized that someone saw them as easy pickings.

Martin Burlington sat at his desk, shirt sleeves pushed up. Beads of sweat pimpled his forehead. An anemic ceiling fan shuffled the stifling July air around his office. His bedroom in the apartment above could bake bread. Suddenly, there was a triple rap on the door, jostling his private investigator shingle. As the young woman entered the room, he jabbed his pencil behind his ear. He liked what he saw but stifled a whistle.

Slender, with long bare legs that started somewhere up inside her flowered skirt. The buttons on her blue blouse strained across the ripeness of her breasts. She approached the chair in front of his desk and waited. He gave a quick nod.

She slid onto the wooden seat, placing her clutch on her lap. "I'm hoping you can help me," she said, imploring him with flecked green eyes.

"With what?" Damn, but her lips looked soft. Thick waves of auburn hair haloed her head.

Squeezing laced fingers, she said, "I need you to find my murderer."

Burlington knitted his brows. "Uh, whose murderer, Miss … uh?"

"Eileen Barrows. Me. What I mean is, I am Eileen Barrows and I was the victim."

The PI leaned back in his swivel chair, bolts groaning from their age and his weight. He locked his hands behind his head, dark circles showing under his armpits. "I gotta say, you certainly look very much alive."

Tears threatened her eyes. "The police don't believe me."

She didn't look the hysterical type. "Well then, you better start at the beginning." Burlington pinched the pencil from his ear, ready to take notes.

"My roommate, Connie, and I shared a room in her grandmother's house in Lewes, not far from Fort Miles. On Saturday nights, we'd borrow the car and drive to a taproom in Dewey Beach. We'd dance, soldiers would buy us drinks, and then we'd go home. We had a ten o'clock curfew. Then, one night, I was killed."

Here it comes. "And which night was that?"

May 15, 1943. A warm spring evening. Eileen heard music over the crunch of the car tires on gravel as Connie steered into a parking space at the Bottle and Cork. Smoke and soldiers spilled from the door. Loud chatter barely beat out the keyboard and drums. Eileen and Connie squeezed through a maze of bodies to get to the bar but were intercepted and pulled onto the dance floor. Hardly room to swing but enough for a slow dance. Later, gin and tonics would offer respite for tired feet.

Thirty minutes before curfew, the friends had one last dance. Turning for the door, Eileen felt Connie grab her hand. With a wink, she slipped Eileen the car keys. "Eugene will see me home."

Eileen took a deep breath and shook her head. *She's asking for trouble.* Eileen was almost to the car when she heard a voice.

"Excuse me."

She swiveled to see a soldier approaching and realized it was Scooter, the guy who had stepped on her feet while dancing. She flashed a quizzical smile.

"Are you going anywhere near Fort Miles? My buddies aren't ready to go back yet; I was hoping to catch a lift."

Indecision was followed by weak rationale. *I'm helping the war effort.* "I'm headed to Lewes. Hop in."

Scooter came alongside the car and stooped down for a moment. Then he yanked open the passenger door and slid in.

Eileen pulled out onto 14A, which would take them up into Rehoboth and then back roads would deliver them to his base. Scooter regaled her with tales of life at Fort Miles. Then, she noticed that the car had started to wobble.

"What's going on?" Eileen blurted, strangling the steering wheel.

"Sounds like a flat tire. Pull over here." He jerked his thumb to the right. The car eased over onto the grass and came to a stop alongside some trees.

"Oh, no. This isn't my car! How will I get home?" Eileen got out and craned her neck, up and down the street, trying to conjure up help.

"Don't worry that pretty little head. Pop the trunk." Scooter loped to the back and peered inside. "We've got a tire, some rags, and an old quilt, but no jack. We'll have to wait 'til some of my buddies are on their way back; they'll be happy to help a damsel in distress."

What bad luck. She started to climb back into the car.

"Tell you what," Scooter said, "Why don't we take a walk until the cavalry arrives?"

Eileen hesitated. "Should we leave the trunk up, so someone will know we need help?"

"Good idea." He led Eileen into the sparse woods. "Darn. I left my wallet on the seat. Don't move." Eileen studied the stars until—*what was that?* She turned to head back to the trees as Scooter came loping into view.

"C'mon. Just a few minutes." He put his arm around her shoulders. "Hey, who better to protect you than a soldier, right?"

"Okay. Fifteen, no more." Scooter put his arm around her waist. Eileen wriggled free. "Did you know this area is a bird refuge?" She clung to the safety of idle chatter. "Silver Lake's just over there."

"Then lead the way."

As she turned, she saw Scooter glance quickly over his shoulder.

"I fought off his advances. I ran into the refuge, but he caught my arm and pulled me to the ground. That's when I screamed. He picked up a rock and smashed it against my head." Eileen reached up and gingerly touched her temple. She swiped at tears. "Maybe it was adrenaline, but I got up and started running. He tripped on a tree root. I made it to the car but collapsed before I could get in and lock the doors."

Burlington wavered between yelling, "You dumb broad!" and offering genuine concern. He leaned forward, cleared his throat, and said, "You're lucky to be alive, but because you are, it's considered assault, not homicide."

Eileen had pulled out a hankie, which she now twisted in her hands. "There's more." She reversed her crossed legs. Burlington's eyes followed the smooth movement. "Apparently, I fell to the ground just as a car was coming up the road. My attacker ran away. The driver called for help on his CB radio. He started pumping on my chest until the ambulance came."

"Did the police inform you of this?"

"No. This is the strange part. I could see it all happening from above. I was looking down at myself, wondering what all the fuss was about, because I felt fine. I saw the ambulance arrive and the medics slide me into it. I saw myself being wheeled into the hospital. I heard the medics tell the staff I was DOA."

"You're telling me you were alive while you were dead?"

"I was dead; that part is true. But then the 'me' on the inside, the part that's not my physical body, started to rotate, faster and faster, until I spun out of myself. I felt so free, of my body and of pain. The police questioned the medics and I heard everything they said, but as soon as the doctor gave a last effort to save me, my heart jumped back to life and my spirit, ghost, whatever, was sucked back into my body. I was in a coma for three days." Eileen's eyes pleaded for belief.

The PI rubbed the stubble on his chin. "Well, no judge will let a man stand trial for murder while his victim is alive and well in the courtroom, but the slimeball does need to be put away for a long while. Let me see—"

"If I may, there's a bit more to my story." Eileen's voice shook. "Ever since I was brought back, I have maintained the ability to leave my body, at any time I choose. At first, I was terrified, but after a few weeks I got the hang of it. I can fly through the air and through walls. I see people, hear conversations, remember details. And then I return to the physical me. I know I can help you find him."

Deep breath, long exhale. "Let's not get carried away. What did he look like? I know you told the cops, but there might be something you inadvertently left out."

"Tall, dark hair, chipped front tooth. But something didn't fit. It kept bothering me. Then I realized, he was different from the other servicemen. He was a loner; the others came and went in small groups. Their uniforms always looked neat and clean. His was as wrinkled as crumpled paper, as if it had been balled up. His shoes were also scuffed, not shined like the others'."

"So, this scumbag could be an imposter, a civilian." Burlington pushed back his chair. "Let me take it from here. I'll be in touch."

"But I could help—"

The PI held up his beefy hand. "No. I don't want any more harm to come to you. Go home."

Eileen gave a small pout but picked up her clutch and stood. "Thank you for believing me."

The detective showed her out the door. He then returned to his desk to consider all he had just heard.

Burlington climbed into his clunker and rumbled onto the street. Sweat poured down the sides of his face, despite the windows being rolled down. He'd start with the scene of the crime.

He parked on the edge of the sanctuary, a spit of land alongside Silver Lake. He took his time, carefully perusing the ground, knowing that two months' time had deteriorated any evidence.

From there, he headed into Dewey, to the Bottle and Cork. It was his lucky day; the bartender on duty had been there the night Eileen Barrows was attacked.

"What can you tell me about the girl, or the guys she danced with? Did she come in with anyone, leave with anyone?" Burlington already knew the answers, but it helped to have witnesses give their versions.

The bartender offered no new info, and no, he couldn't think of anyone who was there that night who could serve as another witness. "The group of GIs is different each weekend because they only get a pass every so often. I might not see any of them twice, if they go to different taverns."

That makes sense, damn it. "Well, can you think of even one face that was familiar to you? Maybe a resident in town?"

"Girls, yes. Men, no."

"I'll take what I can get." Burlington left with two names.

Eileen lay on her bed, frustrated, yet believing that the PI didn't think she was a loon. Her eagerness for mingling on Saturday nights had shifted to an intense impatience as she waited for night to fall. She had not spilled to Connie anything about her excursions, and Connie had no idea that Eileen still went to the Bottle and Cork, only in a different form. No need to get dolled up now.

The sensation of being unhindered, unencumbered, was becoming more familiar as she made her night flights. Hovering above the taproom, questions nagged. How did he get a uniform? Would she recognize him if he were smartly dressed, like the other soldiers? Toward the end of the evening, she saw Connie exit through the door, their friend Patsy now her companion. Maybe Connie was also keeping an eye out for Eileen's attacker. Again, he did not show up. Eileen zoomed back to Lewes, to her body, and arrived well before Connie slumped into the room.

The following day, PI Burlington rumbled up to Lewes, searching for the house with the red shutters. Both potential witnesses lived on the same road that led out to the farm area. The pretty strawberry blonde said she remembered a guy who looked a bit sloppy, and yet, a uniform always looks good, even wrinkled, but no, she did not interact with him. Her friend, the brunette, not as pretty but with a nice smile, said she danced with GI Sloppy, and yes, he stomped on her painted tootsies.

"Anything else?" He was not getting anywhere.

PI Martin Burlington inwardly tried to deny that he was looking forward to seeing his client again. He saw her through the office window and was already on his feet when she entered. With his outstretched arm, he motioned to the same scuffed wooden chair that had previously cradled Eileen's firm posterior. *You cannot be jealous of a chair!* He rolled his huge shoulders as a diversion for his thoughts and reclaimed the seat behind his desk.

"So, here's what we know about the greaseball. He's not who he pretends to be. He is not in the military. He is not stationed at Fort Miles. He's probably in his early twenties, tall, and has a chipped tooth. He's friendly when he needs to be but is really a loner who does not interact with other servicemen. It would be too easy for him to get tripped up on the details of military life." He paused to swipe at the sweat on his brow, inwardly cursing the weather. "Are you with me, so far?"

Eileen gave a sober nod. She, too, patted at the dewy moisture on her temples and in the V of her neckline. Burlington longed to be that hankie.

He harrumphed; back to the matter at hand. "But he's made a mistake in overlooking the condition of his uniform and shoes. He also has a dance signature of stepping on toes."

Eileen gulped in a breath, making her cleavage rise and fall. Burlington saw her catch his stare and her cheeks flamed.

"However," he continued, "we can't turn the dogs loose, just yet. Here's what we don't know: is he local? Does he work nearby? If so, what kind of job and where? And why impersonate a GI?"

"Maybe he wants to be one but can't?" Eileen tossed out.

"You may have something. Uncle Sam needs all the recruits he can get. Therefore, if the dirty dog is not able to enlist, why not? Was he deemed 4F?" Burlington paused and saw the confusion in her eyes. "4F is when the army turns you down because you couldn't pass the physical."

"Oh. So, he could be fuming mad because the army wouldn't take him. Is there a way to check on who's been turned down?"

"I'll look into it. It could be a haystack without a needle, but it's worth a look-see."

Burlington headed to the local recruitment office in George-town.

"Say, can you give me some reasons why you would turn down an eager young man who wanted to serve his country?"

"Have a seat," said the sergeant, who was about the same age as the suspect. He filled out his uniform with an air of confidence, accountability, and character. "Some of the more common reasons are poor eyesight, asthma, flat feet, and heart murmurs. The list goes on, but you get the idea."

"Could I get names and addresses of men who were turned down, say, in the last three years?"

"Access to those records is above my grade. You would have to petition for them, and even then, I don't know if you could get them without a court order."

"Understandable." Burlington pursed his lips. "You've been very helpful. Thank you."

Sweltering humidity made the air a muck of pea soup. Bur-lington chewed his nail as he mulled over this information. He turned onto Rehoboth Avenue, which led to the center of town and its boardwalk. It was late in the day, and he was in the mood for an ice cream cone. By the time he reached the bench to enjoy it, it was already dripping down his paw.

One bench over sat a young woman. On a hunch, he ap-proached, feeling the fool as he licked ice cream off his beefy fingers. "Good afternoon, Miss. I'm investigating a crime and was wondering if you go to taverns?"

"No, I don't drink." She shaded her eyes as she looked up at him.

"Hmmm. Okay. Any chance you go to dances?"

"A few times, at the Henlopen Hotel."

"Ever dance with someone who stepped on your toes?" Burlington pressed.

"No, but my older sister knew someone in high school who did. The girls nicknamed him Pidge."

"Why that?"

She laughed. "Because he was pigeon-toed."

Burlington's heart started racing, his scalp tingling. "Do you remember his name?"

"Darren something."

Burlington jumped in his car, accelerator to the floor. Ask administration for a senior class picture of a guy named Darren! Suddenly, he screeched to a halt and cursed himself. It was summer. The school would be closed.

Eileen hovered inside the Bottle and Cork, again. Maybe he had gone on to another town or been scared off by nearly getting caught. A young woman was leaving, unescorted. Eileen followed her out the door. She canvased the lot with her gaze. Over there, behind the dumpster. He stepped forward to make his move.

"Excuse me, Miss."

No, don't go with him! Eileen tried to warn the girl, but

communication was impossible.

"Sure, hop in."

Her ethereal essence saw Scooter bend down by the side of the car, just as he had done with her. She watched as he made a quick jab with something—a pen knife? No. An ice pick! *No wonder I had a flat tire by the time we reached the lake.*

Eileen was frantic. She had to get help. Within moments, she was back at the house and slid into her body just as Connie walked through the door.

"Connie, call the police! Tell them my attacker has another victim and they're headed to Silver Lake. Don't ask me how I know; just do it." Looking baffled, Connie raced down the stairs.

Eileen grabbed Burlington's business card from her purse and raced downstairs, yanking the phone from Connie as she thanked the officer on the other end of the line.

"Burlington," the PI said, his voice heavy, as if just awoken.

"Mr. Burlington, it's him! He just left the Bottle and Cork with a girl, and he … he stabbed her tire. Please, you have to find her!"

In a flash, Burlington ran out the front door. He floored his clunker, praying it would stay in one piece as he ran stop signs to get to the bird refuge. *What if that's not where he's taking her?* He kept his eyes peeled for an innocent girl driving with a wannabe soldier.

He fishtailed as he skidded around the corner, putting him on Silver Lake Drive. It had been nine minutes since Eileen's call, and several minutes before that when the pair left the taproom. "Go, go, go!" he commanded his rolling tin can, beating the steering wheel. And then, at that moment, he saw a car, parked at an angle, on the grassy shoulder.

Unbeknownst to him, Eileen was hot on his heels, flying at breakneck speed. She looked down as Burlington screeched to a halt, shot across the street, and ran around to the tail of the parked car. The passenger rear wheel was flat.

Burlington fled into the refuge, the moon offering little light. *Watch for tree roots.* When he was midway, he stopped to listen, but the blood pounding in his ears made it difficult. A strained "no" seemed to come from the direction of the lake. Then he heard a yell. *Over there!* He raced out of the sanctuary and onto the lush grass, where he saw two figures wrestling.

"Stop!" Burlington cried, as if it were his own daughter being attacked. "I have a gun." The imposter jumped up, tripping on the pants around his ankles. Pulling them up, he attempted to bolt, but Burlington was on him like a seagull on a crab. He barreled into the guy and slammed him to the ground. In his rage, his hands went around the kid's neck and he started squeezing. Tighter and tighter. The boy gurgled, turned red, clawed at the ever-tightening vice. *This is for Eileen.* And then released his grip.

The young woman had run to the safety of the trees, heaving to catch her breath in between sobs of disbelief. Once he hand-cuffed the imposter, Burlington stumbled over to comfort her.

They heard the siren before they saw lights. "Just in the nick of time, officers," Burlington sneered, as he threw his arm in the direction of Scooter. "I'll see this young lady gets home. You can question her tomorrow."

Afterward, Burlington pulled into his driveway and wasn't surprised to see Eileen. She flew at him, wrapping her arms around his neck, repeating, "Thank you, thank you!"

Exhausted, he reached up and reluctantly pried her arms away from him. He cupped her face in his hands and held her gaze for a moment. Leaning in, he kissed her. On the forehead.

Answers were plentiful once the assailant gave his statement. Burlington filled in Eileen as they left his office to walk along the boards.

"It was as you thought. Darren Birdbrain tried to enlist but was deemed 4F because of being pigeon-toed. He worked as a bellhop at the Henlopen Hotel. That uniform only added to his resentment of not being able to make the cut for the army. His slick alias of 'Scooter' also points to his desperation."

So, how did he get the army uniform?"

"Stole it from a guest at the hotel. A soldier was on a weekend pass, staying there to visit with family from Kansas. The lowlife kept it wadded up in his knapsack. He chose the Bottle and Cork in Dewey because he didn't know anyone down there and felt anonymous in the crush of soldiers who packed the place. He's from Rehoboth, up near Lewes and Fort Miles. I guess being in the shadow of the fort on a daily basis was too much of a blow to his manhood." The PI steered Eileen to a bench.

"You were incredibly brave. I am so grateful to you." She laid her hand on top of his.

They sat for a few comfortable moments. Then he said,

"We did this together, kid. I gotta tell you, I had my doubts about all your flitting and flying all over the place, but I will never doubt you again."

"Well, I think we make a pretty good team." Eileen gave him a coy smile. "How about you take me on as a consultant?"

Burlington laughed. Maybe there was hope for him, after all.

Chris Jacobsen has enjoyed coming to Rehoboth, from the Philadelphia area, ever since it became home for family members a number of years ago.

Chris received a judge's award for her stories in the Rehoboth Beach Reads publications, *The Boardwalk* and *Beach Life*. Last year she was excited to have a story published in *Beach Love*.

In thinking of a story line for *Beach Pulp*, Chris was intrigued when she learned about the real-life murder of an army warrant officer in his home on Silver Lake during World War II. Years later, a diorama was made of the crime scene, complete with victim and murder weapon. It was so detailed that it was used as a training device for the incoming classes of police officers. Today the diorama resides in the Delaware State Police Museum and Education Center in Dover.

WHEN WORLDS COLLIDE

BY J. PATRICK CONLON

The first thing I saw as I walked down Baltimore Avenue to the Black Whale Comic Shop was the words "Listeners Suck!" spray-painted across the door in bright yellow. "Listeners" were what the newspapers called us.

Ever since a strange signal was broadcast around the globe for a week straight, certain people could do amazing things: fly, bend steel, lift cars. Everyone heard the signal, but we were the ones who *listened*. There were those who were envious, those who hated us, even.

I could see piles of comic books strewn haphazardly around the interior of the shop from my vantage point in the doorway. The back wall where the signed editions were displayed was in disarray as well, with a few issues sustaining real damage but most just moved from their places. This looked to be the work of an amateur, but Mentor had not been responding to his communicator. My gut told me this was more than just simple vandalism. As I reached out to move the police tape, a hand fell onto my shoulder.

"Excuse me, sir, but this is an active crime scene."

I glanced over my shoulder at the voice. The Rehoboth Beach Police officer looked no more than twenty. He tried for a severe look, and I almost took pity on him. He was right; this was an active crime scene. But I didn't have time to spare his feelings.

"Son, I have more right to be here than you do. Now, if you don't mind." The hand on my shoulder tightened its grip as I moved to enter the shop again.

"I don't know who you think you are, but …" He tried to put me into an armbar.

I ducked low and pivoted, coming up behind him as my hand snaked around, breaking his hold. I pushed him into the store in front of me, his arm twisted behind his back.

"Release me immediately, sir. Assaulting an officer is a serious offense."

"Son, look up." I pointed with my free hand to the row of comics on the wall above. The issue that hung directly above him was Dr. Dream Issue #1. The titular hero was standing against the backdrop of a psychedelic landscape, nightmarish creatures arrayed around him. He was weaving his hands, body bathed in an iridescent fog. That cover always made me cringe, but the likeness was pretty spot-on.

"Dr. Dream?"

I let him go, and he put some distance between us. Then he turned and examined me.

He took in the rainbow spectacles perched on my forehead and the bright-red trench coat, but his eyes flicked to my hands. They were sheathed in my trademark leather gauntlets. The tubes and lights are just for theatrics; the real danger lies in the tiny hypodermic needles woven into the fabric. With one touch I can pump enough sedative to bring down a rhino.

While he decided how to handle the situation, I took the

lead. "What happened here, and where is Mentor?"

"We received a call about a kid vandalizing the store yesterday," the officer answered.

"And you're just responding to it now? What on earth took you so long?"

"Well, this place belongs to Mentor. Who knocks over Mentor's store? We figured he would take care of the kid, give him a slap on the wrist and send him on his way." The officer shrugged. "We get involved, there are reports to file, child services to call. It has consequences for a kid who probably has enough to worry about."

Made sense. "You have a description of this kid?"

"Better. We found him trying to get this from the bushes around the corner." The patrolman held up a dark brown backpack. "Must've dropped it."

"May I?" I reached for it. The officer tried to hide his flinch from me, but I noticed. I took it from him and opened it. Inside I found several cans of spray paint and a pair of gloves stained with yellow. I would need to tread lightly.

I looked over to the patrol car. A pair of bright-blue eyes glared back at me. There was anger and pain behind that gaze.

I gestured to the officer. "Hey, can you unlock the back?"

He hesitated for a second, and I raised an eyebrow. "You think I can't handle him?" The click of the doors answered my question. Walking around the car, I opened the far door and climbed into the back with him.

"What's your name?"

"You're Dr. Dream, aren't you? Why don't you just put me

under and find out for yourself."

"I could do that," I said, raising a gauntlet and spreading my fingers wide. The boy's eyes locked with mine and I saw that though there was defiance, there was also fear. I lowered my hand. "But I'd rather just talk for now. Tell you what, I'll go first."

"I already know your name, doctor."

"My name is Fred," I said, and saw him narrow his eyes. Fred Thompson was a name I kept from the public as a closely guarded secret.

"*Fred?*"

"Yes. Now, why don't you tell me yours."

"Robbie," he said hesitantly.

"Good to meet you, Robbie." I stretched my hand toward him, and he flinched. This time, my eyes narrowed. "Oh, of course, sorry." I pulled my gauntlet off and reached out again. He took it warily.

"Now, why don't you tell me what happened here?"

"I came back to get my backpack and saw the place was wrecked." He jerked a thumb over his shoulder toward the officer, who was examining the damage in the comic shop. "Then that cop grabbed me and threw me into this car."

"Then that *is* your bag?" I asked with a frown.

"Yeah, so what?"

"Where is Mentor?"

"How should I know?"

"Don't play games with me, Robbie," I growled. Deep down, I knew I shouldn't be coming down so hard on him, but he was old enough to know better, and Mentor was a dear friend.

"Wait, you think I did something to Mentor?" The anger rushed out of him in a thick wave.

"Well, you did say it was your backpack." I softened my voice as much as I could, but the steel was still there.

His eyes narrowed and then went wide. "Okay, I did paint the message, but I don't know anything about Mentor."

"Why come back so late?"

"I came back after I was sure he'd closed the shop and gone home. I hate Listeners, but I'm not foolish enough to try to take one on."

"But perhaps foolish enough to work with someone who could."

"C'mon, Fred," the anger was entirely replaced with fear now.

I pulled my glove back on and sighed. I reached out again. "I wish I could take your word for it, but I'm going to have to see it for myself."

As my hand closed on his wrist, I willed the gauntlet to dispense a small amount of sedative. His eyes grew wide and then drooped closed almost immediately. I knocked on the window, and the officer let me out of the police car. He looked at the kid and back to me.

"Dr.?"

"Watch over my body while I enter Robbie's, officer." With that, I turned back to Robbie. Closing my eyes, I concentrated, and felt the familiar pull on my mind. This is why everyone flinches when I reach for them. Some people fly. Some bend bars. I, however, enter your subconscious. See what's inside your mind. I call it the dreamscape. It's where we all go when we sleep, but I have complete control of every detail. It's what makes me the most feared of the Phenomenal Five. I slid from my body and floated into his small sleeping form, determined to find out where Mentor had gone and prayed that I had not arrived too late.

I opened my eyes and found myself sitting on one of the benches along the boardwalk facing the ocean. Looking down, I saw the telltale glow around myself that signified I had successfully entered the dreamscape of Robbie's mind. I got up and turned away from the surf. I was outside the Victoria Restaurant, and Robbie was walking along the boardwalk toward Baltimore Avenue. The backpack was slung over his shoulder, and he was moving quickly. I willed myself invisible and followed close behind. He doubled back several times, only serving to make himself look more obvious.

I watched as he sprayed the message across the front door. I raised a hand, freezing the scene, and searched the shadows for anyone Robbie was working with. There was no indication of anyone. A wave of my hand and time accelerated. After Robbie finished the words, he hurled a rock through a window.

"I'll show you!" he cried, tears streaming down his face.

A loud clap of thunder came from inside the comic shop, causing Robbie to drop his bag. I strained to see what was happening inside the shop, but the perspective spun away as he turned and ran for the street. I froze the dream again.

The look on Robbie's face was of sheer terror. I wasn't sure I understood what had happened between Mentor and this boy; however, I did know that whatever was happening in the comic shop had nothing to do with him.

I ran the dream back slowly. The perspective swung to face the shop. I walked over and peered in the window. The inside was filled with a bright white light that began to shrink into itself. As it did, the outline of a man's legs appeared, sheared clean at the waist. I drew in a sharp breath. If those belonged to Mentor, then I had been too late to save him.

Then the light receded further, and Mentor was spat out of a swirling vortex. I exhaled. It was teleportation, not a disintegration. That meant there was hope that whoever had taken Mentor had not had a chance to kill him yet. I began to close my eyes to end the dream when the portal pulled into itself and coalesced into a symbol. I snapped my eyes back open. The swirling purple vortex with the laughing skull that hung in the air before my friend was one I knew all too well.

I closed my eyes and focused my will on exiting Robbie's mind. Mentor did not have much time left, but Robbie had given me what I needed to find him. The dreamscape collapsed around me until all that was left in my mind was a single name: Erik Tangarian. He and Mentor had been friends once. The same signal that had given Mentor his power to inspire had driven Erik insane. The only thing that remained of Erik's old life was his memory of Mentor. I guess that's what gave Erik his name. I was going up against Professor De-Mentor.

After leaving Robbie in the capable hands of the Rehoboth

Beach police, I decided to take a walk along the boardwalk. I knew that Mentor was in trouble, but if I merely rushed around, I would never find him in time. There were apparently some issues between Robbie and Mentor, but they would have to wait.

The issue at hand now was where to find De-Mentor. Thankfully, he was predictable for an insane evil genius. Even though Mentor had been teleported from the shop, Erik wouldn't have taken him far. His obsession was such that he would want to defeat him near his home.

I thought about all the landmarks that De-Mentor might use against my old friend. Dr. De-Mentor was always a fan of using the items from their past against Mentor. While Dolles' iconic sign was the definitive landmark of the town, Mentor didn't really like popcorn or taffy. The distinct smell of tomato and mozzarella drifted from Grotto as I passed. Mentor loved pizza, but he was much more partial to Louie's.

Several hours had passed, and I found myself back in front of Mentor's store. There were still no clues as to where my friend had been taken. I reached up and pulled the spectacles from my forehead. I stared at the swirling rainbow of colors that shifted and spun within the lenses. A small movement caught my eye, and I put them back in place and flexed my fingers. I walked to the corner of the cul-de-sac and took a steadying breath.

I leapt forward, fingers splayed, preparing to unleash a full spray of sedative. Robbie jumped from the steps, and something fell to the ground. Before he could grab it, I scooped it up. It was a Mentor comic book. My face grew hot. I was so sure that Robbie had had nothing to do with Mentor's disappearance, but here he was at the scene again, mocking me with that comic.

"What are you doing here, Robbie?"

"I dunno."

"Yes, you do."

"Okay, fine. I come here because of how it makes me feel." He snatched at the comic and the cover tore, exposing the inner page. I saw the bold swirling *M* that marked Mentor's signature. Then I saw the rest of the letters. *YERS*. Mentor had signed this comic with his real name, *MYERS*. Everyone knew this was Mentor's shop. But no one knew Jacob Myers. Jacob would not have entrusted that name to just anyone. This boy was special.

"You come here because of the inspiration aura that Jacob has."

His eyes widened in fear at my mention of Mentor's real name.

"It's okay. I've known Jake for many years. He inspired me to join the Phenomenal Five, after all."

"I always feel like I could do anything when I'm here. It's why I'm here now."

"Now?" I furrowed my brow.

"Robbie, do you feel inspired right now?"

"Yeah."

I grabbed my spectacles and pulled them back into place. The inside of the shop lit up with crackling lines of energy.

I had been such a fool. I had thought De-Mentor would keep him close, but I had not realized how close. Jacob was still inside the shop. The comic fell from my hand. Robbie grabbed it, gingerly closing the cover and placing it carefully into his backpack.

"What's wrong?"

"You should get out of here." I flexed my gloves, bright purple beads of liquid springing from my fingertips. "Mentor is still here. But so is Professor De-Mentor and he will not hesitate to hurt you."

"Professor De-Mentor?" Robbie stood, brandishing his backpack before him.

"Go!" I shouted, as I stepped into the shop, my gaze locked on the swirling maelstrom of light. I took another step forward.

"I know you're there, Erik. And I know you can see me." The light began to pulse and throb. "What's the matter? Only interested in Mentor? Have you forgotten the humiliating defeats I handed you time and time again?" The wind began to pick up in the shop. "Well, I suppose it's for the best that you stay hidden. Goodness knows it would take a real genius to defeat both Dr. Dream and Mentor. Your dumb luck is the only reason you captured Mentor."

A portal ripped open, nearly knocking me from my feet. A large glowing hand reached out to grasp me.

"I am a real genius!" a voice boomed, as I was swept from my feet and yanked through the portal.

When I regained consciousness, I found myself bound tightly to a large metallic pillar. The air smelled heavily of ozone, and the thrum of electricity was palpable. The room around me was almost entirely metallic, with a second pillar much like the one I was tied to dominating the center. There were many small work tables, and every flat surface was covered with test tubes, beakers, books, and all manner of strange contraptions.

"Finally awake, are we?"

I strained to look over my shoulder at the source of the voice, but my restraints held me fast.

"Professor, I expected something more from you than a mere pocket dimension."

A rustle of cloth and several loud bangs sounded behind me. Professor De-Mentor then stepped around the edge of my vision and stood in the center of the room. His hair was swept back haphazardly from his face, dark bronze welding goggles covering his eyes. A black lab coat billowed out behind him, but it was his hands that held my gaze. He wore my gauntlets.

Grinning wickedly, he flexed a gloved hand inches from my face. "I think they look better on me, wouldn't you agree?"

I struggled, but my bonds held me fast. De-Mentor seemed to revel in my exertion. My eyes darted around the room, looking for anything I could use against him. De-Mentor turned away after several moments, cackling.

"Struggle all you want, Doctor, those bonds are more than a match for you." He gestured to the other pillar. "Just like they were for him." Mentor hung from his restraints, body limp and motionless. I had arrived too late. Then I saw Mentor's chest rise and fall slightly.

"What exactly do you hope to gain from this, Erik? Ambushing a couple of heroes doesn't exactly scream genius."

"Why, I plan to steal your powers, of course!" He threw his arms wide.

"Seriously? That's your ingenious plan?"

"What's wrong, doctor?" He waved a gauntleted hand in front of my face. "Are you afraid?"

I laughed despite myself. "Afraid? Of something impossible? Not really."

"It is not impossible! I have devised a way of doing exactly that." He walked back over to the draped table in the middle of the room, then whipped the fabric off, revealing a large cylindrical object.

"What is that supposed to be?"

"I'm so glad you asked. This," he said, as he thrust it over his head, "is my signal transmogrifier."

"Your what?" I glanced over at Mentor. He still hung limply, but his hand moved slightly. He was playing possum.

"My signal transmogrifier," he shouted. "It allows me to pull powers out of a Listener and store them. Then I simply reverse the polarity and point it at myself to transfer them."

I rolled my eyes at him. "Let me guess. You used it on Mentor already and have his powers."

"Well, no." De-Mentor's face fell, then twisted with rage. "I've just completed it. And it is so fitting for your powers to be the first in my collection." He pointed the cylinder at me. "Once I have your powers, I will enter Mentor's dreams and tear his mind asunder from the inside. Quite inspiring, don't you think?"

Though I wasn't convinced that De-Mentor could take my powers, I wasn't keen to find out. I struggled again with my bonds while he took aim. When the machine started to vibrate, I closed my eyes and steeled myself.

A loud thump sounded, and I opened my eyes. De-Mentor was toppling backward, a black bookbag pasted to his face. I watched as Robbie removed the gag from Mentor's mouth.

"Get away from him!" De-Mentor screamed, and a dagger appeared in his hands. He threw it, end over end, and it crashed into Robbie just as the gag fell from Mentor's face.

Mentor sucked in a deep breath, and I wished I could put my hands over my ears, because I knew what was coming. This was a power he rarely used, and few had heard before. Mentor shouted and his scream filled every inch of the room. I was instantly filled with despair. I felt the weight of every lousy decision fall upon my shoulders. Tears streamed down my face as the chasm of my failures opened before me. Nothing mattered now, I had already lost. I was able to keep my eyes open just long enough to see Dr. De-Mentor collapse on top of the transmogrifier. Then everything went black.

A hand fell on my shoulder and shook me gently. Opening my eyes, I was greeted by the exhausted face of Mentor. He looked battered from his ordeal, but he smiled, nonetheless.

"I thought this was the part where I save you," I muttered, the lingering effect of Mentor's desolation wave causing my voice to waver.

"Well, doctor, you finding me allowed me to save you, so I think that makes us even."

I returned his smile, then looked around frantically. "Where is Robbie? Is he all right?" I started to stand, but Mentor's hand on my shoulder kept me rooted to the ground.

"Relax, Fred." Mentor gestured behind him to where Robbie lay.

"It's a good thing Erik is a mad scientist and not a mad soldier. The handle hit Robbie in the head, but just knocked him out."

"He's the one who vandalized your shop, you know."

"I know." Jacob frowned.

"Do you know why he did it?"

"I do." Jacob sighed. "But it is not my place to discuss it."

I shrugged and looked over to where De-Mentor lay in a heap. What was left of the transmogrifier lay crushed beneath him.

"You think that would have worked?"

"Did any of Erik's contraptions really work?" Mentor shrugged. "I doubt it. Everyone knows that the signal is not something you can harness. If it were, where are all the new heroes and villains?"

"You're probably right," I groaned, as he helped me to my feet. I walked over to De-Mentor and retrieved my gauntlets. I slipped them back on and flexed the fingers.

"Let's get Robbie home."

I stood outside a small beach house on Laurel Street. Robbie stood beside me and shuffled his feet.

"You aren't going to tell my parents what I did, are you?"

"That depends on what you tell me about it."

"It was a dumb thing to do, I know that now."

"I'm not interested in whether you learned your lesson, Robert."

His jaw tightened at the mention of his full name. "I did it because of what Mentor said to me."

My eyebrows raised. "Oh, what did Jacob say?"

"He said …" Tears began to well in Robbie's eyes. "He said I couldn't be a hero."

I felt my own jaw tighten at the words. I knew how Robbie felt. Being able to enter peoples' dreams and influence their thoughts was a power that no one ever believed could be used for good. How many times had I been told that I could never be trusted? That villainy was only one wrong decision away. I placed my hand on Robbie's shoulder.

"Robbie, you already are a hero." He looked up at me, hope filling his face. "Your actions put yourself at considerable risk. And you saved both Mentor and me from Professor De-Mentor. You showed great courage. However—"

"I'm not a Listener. I know." His face fell, and he started to turn away. I pulled him around to face me.

"However, you will need some pretty fancy equipment if you're going to be my sidekick."

"Seriously?"

"Yeah, we'll need a name for you, though." I thought for a moment. "Dream Lad?" I shook my head.

"Can I fly? I've always wanted to fly."

"I suppose I can ask Professor Titanium to make you a rocket pack."

"Ooh! I know what my name will be." He smiled widely.

"I think I do too," I said, throwing an arm around him. "Now let's go figure out how to convince your parents."

The ruins of the transmogrifier still lay strewn about the floor of the pocket dimension. The room was empty and barren, awaiting Professor Titanium and his crew to sweep it clean and reseal the portal in the comic shop.

A loud resonating hum shattered the silence of the room. The shadow of the pillar Mentor had been tied to began to stretch and distort, slowly solidifying into a blurry figure. The black mass slid across the floor to the wreckage of the transmogrifier, thick tendrils probing. After several moments, it withdrew, holding a small microcassette. It then turned and melted back into the pillar, leaving the lab in silence once more.

J. Patrick Conlon is a genre fiction author currently living in Bear, Delaware. He is a member of the Written Remains Writers Guild as well as a partner in Oddity Prodigy Productions. His writing focuses on fantasy and speculative history themes. Patrick's work has appeared in anthologies and magazines, most notably in *A Plague of Shadows*, a collection of haunted tales published by Smart Rhino. You can reach him on his website at www.jpatrickconlon.com, or on twitter at @JPConlonDE. When not writing, he is tirelessly marketing for his amazingly talented wife, Marcella Harte, who is the award-winning illustrator behind *The Mermaid in Rehoboth Bay*, a children's book published by Cat & Mouse Press.

HOOK, LINE, AND SINK HIM

BY MARIA MASINGTON

It started last year when we went to the Blue Hen Theater on Rehoboth Avenue to see *Wedding Present*, starring Cary Grant. It got worse when we read "Edward and Wallis Wed" in a June copy of the Baltimore Sun. All I know is that the proverbial matrimonial ball started rolling, and by August 1937, a certain fella had used Ma Bell to ring a certain filly's father to request her hand in marriage.

Now I sit here, in my favorite juice joint, Dewey Beach's own Bottle n' Cork Taproom, which was Jack's Café until my buddy Harry—who sold my parents their abode—and his lovely wife, Ginger, bought the place last year. No more chugging coffin varnish, now that the laws have changed, and we can drink our hooch legally in a high-class establishment. I ignore the stares I often get, holding court here on my favorite stool, which I guess, as of tomorrow, I'll be trading for a place of honor at a kitchen table. I watch some of the locals drinking that new canned beer, never having tried one myself, afraid it would taste like fizzy tin.

The "band," which is just an organ and drum set, is off for the night, so my favorite crooner Bing Crosby sings "Pennies from Heaven" from the jukebox, while the barkeep sticks his nose in my potatoes and says, "Isn't it time you scram? You have a big day tomorrow."

"Bring me a sidecar," I holler, anxious for that wonderful elixir of Cognac and lemon to wet my whistle, as the hourly countdown begins. I am supposed to make my big appearance at St. Peter's Church in Lewes tomorrow morning.

"So, does this make you the ball or the chain?" he quips.

"Not sure, buddy, but I'm behind the eight ball on this one. How the heck did this happen to me? I feel like I'm going off to the big house, instead of marital bliss. What if at heart I'm just a down-on-my-luck boozehound puttin' in days at the telephone company?"

"Maybe you better pass on this last snort and go tell your betrothed how you feel, before you ruin a life," says Herbert, the off-duty Rehoboth Beach lifeguard to my left.

"Aw, shut your yap! Hit me up bartender," I say. "Where's Miss Ginger? Maybe a nice dame like that would understand me. Let me spill it, sing like a canary, tell her all my fears."

"I hear ya," says Herbert, "and I hate to see some poor sap ruin his life over a skirt, but it happens every day. Maybe you could make a clean sneak, take those long get-away sticks of yours and walk right past the church, or drive through the night to Baltimore, never to be heard from again. All the hens would cluck about being left at the altar; someone sympathetic might stand up and take your place in a month or two!"

"Another giggle juice," I shout, wondering to myself, how do you fall in love with someone's voice? But that's how the story goes. My voice was the clincher and after we met, all bets were off. Granted, there's attraction there, maybe even some affection, but I still feel like I'm losing my freedom, like this is what a twenty-two-year-old adult's supposed to do, whether they want to or not. Next thing you know there'll be house payments, and babies, and oh, jeez, should I order a third? I don't care about how well the yard is mowed, or about new kitchen curtains, or worst of all, relatives coming to visit. I like my life as it is.

"What's the story, morning glory?" A local cop plops onto the stool to my right, wrapping his big meat hook around a Pimm's Rangoon, which is considered a lady's drink in this joint, even though it's just gin and cucumber, which are not particularly girly. "Just think, tomorrow you'll be married to that pip, pitchin' woo on the beach … unless you pass out at the altar. Let me get ya some pickled eggs or a ham sandwich to absorb some of that booze, so you'll look your swanky best tomorrow!"

"You guys are a barrel of monkeys," I say. "If I didn't know better, I'd think you were jealous." But really, I do know better since they're all "happily" married, spending as much time as they can bellied up to either side of the bar, complaining about their wives, when just a few years ago they were dizzy with the dames! Oh, how quickly those Janes went from being the cat's meow to bug-eyed Bettys in their old men's bull sessions. The barkeep slides me a pack of Luckies and I light one up.

"Don't blow your wig," he jokes. "The minute the priest says it's okay to lay a honey cooler on each other, you'll feel better."

"Yeah," I scowl, "like Judas, sealing his fate with a kiss."

"All right," says the barkeep, "before you get boiled as an owl, let's get you home." The lifeguard offers to give me a lift back to my parents' home in Lewes, just a block from the church. "We don't need you wandering off into the swamps of Dewey."

Then Harry plays the same song he plays on the jukebox every time I make tracks. Lead Belly belts out "Goodnight, Irene" through the bar each night as I slip, or sometimes stumble, out into the crisp September beach air. I pull out a Lincoln to pay my tab, but Miss Ginger walks in from the back room and says, "Keep your money, honey. Tonight is on us. You'll be the butterfly's boots tomorrow. Congratulations!"

By noon the next day, I'd have on shoes that pinched my feet and a ring that claimed my finger. I nod, climb off the barstool, and head toward the door. Before I leave, I turn around and ask aloud the question we'd all been wondering about. "Hey gents, isn't it usually *the fella* who feels this way?"

"Yeppers," said the barkeep. "Don't worry, Irene, you'll make a beautiful bride."

Maria Masington is a poet, essayist, spoken word artist, and short story writer from Wilmington, Delaware. Her work has appeared in multiple journals and anthologies, including *Beach Nights*, published by Cat & Mouse Press. Maria is a member of the Written Remains Writers Guild and is active in the Delaware and Philadelphia art scenes. She freelances as an emcee at local open mic nights, promoting both beginning and established writers. *Beach Pulp* gave Maria an opportunity to explore 1930s gender roles and stereotypes of "fellas" and "fillies" in a very fun way!

Steve Myers is an award-winning cartoonist and graphic designer who lives in Bear, Delaware. He spends his days working as a search engine optimization professional, and his evenings running a hyperlocal news website in Lower Merion Township, Pennsylvania. In between all that, he draws comics and cartoons, including *The Adventures of Superchum*, which can be found at www.superchum.com. He learned the craft of producing comic books when he was a production intern at Valiant Comics in the late 1990s, getting introduced to everything from paper quality to color separations from professionals such as Bob Layton, Bob Hall, and Don Perlin. His illustration work has appeared in newspapers from Lansdale, Pennsylvania, to the Hong Kong edition of the *Wall Street Journal*.

MOONWALKER

BY DAVID COOPER

Tawny hid among the rushes, standing as still as the pool at her feet. She watched the reflections of taller girls with carefully braided and ribbon-bound hair cross the bridge above her on their way to school.

The girls stared into cell phones. Spoke over each other. None really paid attention to anything beyond their small screens, but Tawny knew if she emerged, cell phones would disappear into pockets.

Aimless talking would become teasing about Tawny's worn jeans, lack of makeup, or this week's new pimple.

Teasing from girls who had more. Who had mothers.

Tawny whispered a wish to be in Rehoboth at her aunt's cottage, sitting by the water, listening to the surf, feeling the breeze, and watching boats drift into the distance.

The mean girls had crossed the bridge, but Tawny's gaze remained on the pool in front of her. Her foot rose and hung over its glassy surface. Inches separated her sneaker's thin rubber sole from the muddy bottom.

Ripples spread from a dip of her toe.

Without thinking, Tawny leaned forward, stepping flat-footed into the water. Her faded pink sneaker sank into brown silt. The stink of manure runoff from the town's farms wafted up from the stream.

Why do I do that? she thought.

Tawny pulled up her sneaker, and it made a sucking-glurp sound. She would suffer a soggy, creek-smelling foot and the teasing it would bring for the rest of the school day—again.

Maybe those girls are right.

A salty Rehoboth morning breeze woke Tawny from a nightmare she couldn't quite remember, but the mean girls had played roles in it. Caws from gulls reassured her she wouldn't see the bubblegum monsters for another three months.

She lay in the loft of her aunt Cassandra's cottage enjoying the breeze from an open window. A large black fly buzzed by her nose then landed on her aunt's marine biology degree, which was hanging on the wall.

If I could be more like Aunt Cassandra, those girls wouldn't pick on me.

Hushed words from her aunt and grandmother rose from downstairs along with the smell of waffles. Food and low voices—maybe secrets—drew Tawny from bed to the worn wooden steps. She moved slowly, avoiding the creaky spots.

"She needs to know this part of our family," Tawny heard her aunt say. "She's already asking questions. You've seen the way she looks at the water."

Tawny sat on the bottom step, around the corner from the kitchen and its rickety table where the three of them ate each morning.

"Not yet," she heard her grandmother say.

"We were younger than Tawny when we made our first rescue."

We? thought Tawny. *Is she talking about my mother?*

"And you shouldn't have. I should never have told you at all."

"You know it wasn't your fault."

"She'd still be here, wouldn't she?"

"It's who we are, Mom."

"No. It's a curse. It's *our* curse."

Tawny's aunt must have realized their voices had become too loud, because she whispered, "You told us we couldn't run from it. We'd always be drawn back. And, you were right."

"It's not Tawny's time, yet."

"Let's let Tawny decide."

"She's not your daughter."

Tawny turned the corner into the kitchen.

Her aunt winced, then looked down into her coffee.

"Good morning, sweetheart," said Tawny's grandmother. "Waffles and syrup are on the counter."

Tawny moved toward the food.

"All I'm saying—" Cassandra began.

"Not now," Tawny's grandmother said.

"We'll have enough moon tonight."

"I said," Tawny's grandmother smacked her coffee cup on the table, "not now."

Tawny parked her bike near the lifeguard station along the boardwalk, then collected smooth and shiny pebbles as she walked along the beach. She knew she could find her aunt at The Coffee Mill, which was tucked in an alley near the bookstore.

Coffee's sweet-earth aroma reached Tawny when she turned from the sidewalk's bleached tan concrete slabs onto the alley's worn red and brown bricks.

A small bell rang as she opened The Coffee Mill's door and stepped up to a display case of cookies, muffins, and Danishes dotted with blueberries. Behind the case, racks of plastic containers held coffee beans in shades of red, brown, and tan as varied as the hues of the bricks in the alley.

"Hi, Riggs," Tawny said to a graying man pecking away at a cash register.

He lowered spectacles from his face, letting them hang from a chain around his neck. "Tawny! Your aunt told me you were back with us." He turned to a young man working in the kitchenette to his right. "Make an iced chocolate for Tawny."

"Thanks, Riggs." Tawny spotted her aunt at a corner table, her mousy brown hair (a family trait Tawny knew too well) twisted into an untidy bun. Her nose was buried in yellowed and crinkling maps and charts.

"Aunt Cassandra." Tawny spilled a handful of pebbles onto the papers. "Take a look at these."

Her aunt looked up, as if her thoughts had been pulled from some distant land. "Huh? Oh, those are lovely."

"Will you be tagging turtles tonight? Or counting migrating birds?"

Cassandra thought for a moment. "Neither, actually." She pulled another chair to her table and patted it for Tawny to join her. "Remember when your grandmother and I were talking this morning?"

Tawny dropped her chin and moved some of the pebbles around the maps with her finger.

"Okay," Cassandra said, "when we were arguing."

Tawny nodded.

Cassandra joined Tawny in moving the pebbles absently about the table. "I want you to help me tonight."

Tawny's heart jumped. She looked up from the pebbles. "Will Grandma let me?"

Cassandra sighed. "I'm still working on that. Take a nap this afternoon. Don't play too much. We'll be out late." Cassandra reached behind Tawny's hair, squinting at the faded tag on her T-shirt. "I need to get you some clothes for tonight. Still a small, or are you a medium, now?"

"I don't know."

"Pant size?"

Tawny shrugged.

"Well, I have my job cut out for me, then." Cassandra gathered and rolled her papers then slid the bundle into a long cardboard tube.

Riggs approached with Tawny's iced chocolate.

Cassandra smiled at him and said, "We'll see you tonight."

Riggs stopped mid-stride. "We'll?"

"Yep," Cassandra said.

"Both of you?" His brow furled, and he glanced down at Tawny.

"Yes, Riggs. Both of us."

Riggs forced a smile. "Big night for you, then, Tawny." He handed her the drink. "You've grown up so fast."

Tawny tried to nap on the cottage porch. She had curled up on a blanket draped over a wide wicker seat, but tossed restlessly, unable to let go of her excitement.

I could be a marine biologist. She thought about the college bumper stickers on her aunt's Jeep. *Cassandra could help me. I could go to the same college. That's only six years away.*

Her heart sank. *Six years?* She swallowed hard. *Six years of the mean girls?*

She needed to think about something else.

"The Coffee Mill closed hours ago. Why are we here?" Tawny asked, while tugging at the black rubber-like material of her pants and shirt.

Cassandra wore the same outfit, like they were superheroes from a movie.

Her aunt chuckled. "Those will stretch a bit and the itching will go away. Next time, I'll give you some lotion to put on first. Sorry. I wasn't thinking."

The dark and silent brick alley felt narrow, and the buildings on either side seemed to close in around Tawny. The coffee shop was dark, but Cassandra knocked on the door.

Riggs appeared and motioned for them to enter. "You got a beautiful night." He locked the door then led them behind the counter. A small lamp cast a faint glow from the kitchenette where he made coffee and sandwiches. "You sure this is her time, Cassandra?"

"Very sure. It's who we are."

Riggs lifted two backpacks onto the counter, one larger than the other. He reached into the large one and pulled out a tightly packed bundle of rubber tubing attached to a shiny silver cylinder. "Just got this. Better than the old emergency raft. It has a set of lights, repair kit, and built-in bailing pump. The lights are LEDs and should last for days. The whole thing inflates in less than—"

Cassandra put her hand on Riggs' cheek, cutting him off, then took the bundle. "You know we don't go that far, anymore."

"Currents," Riggs said. "And storms pop up so suddenly these days."

Cassandra nodded and returned the compressed raft to the backpack.

Tawny flashed a smile. "Are we going out on a boat?"

Cassandra shook her head.

"You both have new flashlights," Riggs continued. "The big steel ones can be used for self-defense, like—"

"Like you showed me." Cassandra put her hands on her hips. "How many times have I done this, Riggs?"

He put up his hands, said, "I know, I know," and walked over to the sink where he retrieved two thermoses. "This one's your coffee, Cassandra."

Cassandra reached for it.

"It's called Jamaican Me Crazy," he said.

Tawny took the other thermos.

"Hot chocolate," he said.

Tawny opened hers and took a sip. "Thanks!"

Riggs walked them to the door. "Text me the moment your feet touch sand."

"I thought you said we're not going out on a boat?" Tawny stuffed her thermos into the smaller backpack.

Cassandra touched Riggs's arm lightly. "We'll be fine. Go home. You don't have to wait for us."

Tawny followed her aunt down Rehoboth's side streets. They passed behind Funland with its big metal rides dark and still like sleeping dinosaurs. When they reached Silver Lake, they cut toward the beach.

Sweat matted Tawny's bangs to her forehead. She wanted to jump into the cool June water, but her aunt stopped them just beyond the rolling surf's reach.

"Where's the boat?" Tawny asked.

Cassandra stared at the moon, a full one, slightly obscured by a long, thin cloud. When the clouds cleared its face, she closed her eyes and turned her palms down toward the sand.

Everything fell silent.

The surf didn't just calm. The clouds didn't just clear from the sky. Waves hung curled in the air. Clouds hovered motionless.

A chill shot down Tawny's spine. "What's happening?" She

hugged herself. "What happened to the waves?"

Cassandra opened her eyes. "Do you see where the moon-light shines on the water?"

Tawny nodded. "Yeah, I guess."

Cassandra walked onto the water as if it were glass. "Follow me." She stepped over a small wave and climbed over a chest-high breaker farther from the shore. "It's okay. Just stay on the water reflecting the moonlight."

Tawny shook her head. "No. I can't."

"You can. You're a moonwalker, Tawny."

"I'm a what?" Tawny raised her boot over the stilled ocean water, and the moments of stepping into the creek near her school, the times she had spaced-out, flashed through her mind.

Tawny's foot touched the water. This time, the water didn't yield. She realized why she had stood by the creek so often. Why she had suffered soggy sneakers on so many days. "I'm standing on water!"

Cassandra turned to face Tawny. "Come out here with me." Her teeth gleamed in the moonlight.

Tawny walked to where the water should have been knee deep. She bounced lightly and then jumped up and down. "I'm really standing on water."

"We have a lot to do." Cassandra continued beyond the breakers until the ocean became small blue-black hills stretching endlessly to a dark horizon. "Just stay on the moonlit water."

Tawny took a few tentative steps, walked, and then ran to catch up with her aunt. "Is this frozen?" She crouched to feel the smooth, hard ocean. "It's not cold."

"The moonlight makes us a bridge." Cassandra took a few steps to her left, reached into a side pocket on her bag, and pulled out some coins. She tossed one beyond the moonlight reflecting from the water around her, and the coin made a plop. "If we go beyond the light, we'll fall into the water."

Tawny started toward where the coin hit the water.

"It's best to stay back, at least a few yards."

"What about the clouds? Or if the moon sets?"

"As long as we stay on the bridge, we're moving between moments. We'll have more than enough time."

"Time for what?"

Cassandra turned and peered down the moonlit bridge.

"What is it?" asked Tawny.

"The answer to your question." Cassandra hurried farther into the ocean.

Tawny followed and saw a large gull flopping on the bridge.

Cassandra knelt beside the bird. To Tawny's surprise, her aunt lifted it and cradled it in her arms.

"She's swallowed something," her aunt said. "There's string hanging from her mouth. Do you see it?"

Tawny stepped closer. A frayed and soggy string hung from the gull's beak.

"It's okay, little one, hold still," Cassandra said to the gull. "We're going to help you." She turned its head toward Tawny. "See if you can get that string with your fingers."

"It'll bite me."

"Gulls don't have teeth, and she won't try to peck you, either. Just don't scare her."

"Scare *her*?" Tawny tapped her chest. "*I'm* scared."

"Tawny, we need to help her. That's why we're here."

Tawny reached for the string, and the gull opened wide, as if understanding what she planned to do. "I have it."

"Okay, pull gently. Don't stop. I think I know what she's choking on."

Tawny pulled and the gull made a terrible, almost human, gagging sound. A small, fleshy object tied to the end of the string popped from the bird's mouth. The gull cawed several times, clearing its throat, and then Cassandra released it into the night.

"She probably swooped down and scooped up a chicken neck someone was using to catch crabs," Cassandra said.

"So, we're here to help birds?"

"Not just birds. Let me show you something. You know how you can swirl your fingers in the bathtub to make little whirlpools?" Cassandra, still kneeling, passed her fingers over the solid ocean in wide circles. Hard water became soft, then liquefied, swirling round and round. She lifted her fingers and flicked water at Tawny.

Tawny flinched. The cold drops tasted salty on her lips.

"We can open these holes in the bridge to get to …" Cassandra pointed. "Look, over there. A turtle."

Tawny followed Cassandra about twenty yards then looked down at her aunt's feet. Just under the clear surface, a sea turtle stroked its flippers to keep steady. Its glassy eyes blinked at the humans towering above it.

Tawny asked, "How could you see him from all the way over there?"

"Do you know it's a him, or are you guessing?"

Tawny knelt on the hardened water. Squinted at the turtle. "I know it's a boy. I don't know how, really. I just know. There's something wrong with him, isn't there?"

Cassandra nodded. "Open a hole to get to him, like I showed you."

"Me?"

"Well, he isn't going to do it."

Tawny moved her hand in circles. Her fingers brushed the smooth cool surface, circle after circle, yet nothing happened. "What am I doing wrong?"

"You're not doing anything wrong. You just don't believe you can do it."

"I don't understand."

"It's a mindset, Tawny. A way of thinking. What is real and what you believe are connected. One affects the other."

The turtle flapped its flippers, bonking its head against the underside of the bridge, as if it were stuck under ice. Tawny sighed and looked into the turtle's eyes. It made soft whimpering noises in her mind.

"It's all about what you believe," Cassandra said.

Tawny made circles again. Imagined a whirlpool. The surface began to give, a wiggly Jell-O under her touch.

"You're doing it, Tawny. Stay focused. Concentrate."

"It's working!"

The Jell-O turned to water. The turtle popped its head into the night air.

"Pick him up gently," Cassandra said. "He's hurt, some-where."

Tawny reached under its belly, lifting and cradling the tur-tle as if it were a cat. "There's a hook in his back leg. A real big one."

"Hold him still." Cassandra stroked his head. "It's a treble hook with sharp prongs, and he's got two big ones pushed through his skin."

The turtle kept its glistening-brown marble eyes on Tawny.

"He likes you." Cassandra worked the hook gently back and forth. "More importantly, he trusts you."

"But, he shouldn't. Why didn't he swim away when I got close?"

"Remember when Riggs asked me if you were ready?"

Tawny smiled into the turtle's face, putting her nose against his. "Uh huh."

The hook came free. Tawny fumbled with the squirming turtle for a moment.

"Well, this is what Riggs meant."

"Does Riggs do this?"

Cassandra shook her head. "Only the women in our family. Grandma, your mother, you, and me. Maybe there are other families, too, but I don't know of any."

The turtle slapped its flippers against the sides of its shell.

"You should put him back," Cassandra said. She knelt by the hole, waited for Tawny to place the turtle into the water, and circled her fingers to close the opening. "Always close the holes you open."

"Why?"

"You can fall. If you hit your head, the bridge can collapse."

"Did you ever fall into a hole?"

Cassandra put her hand to her mouth. "Just always close the holes you make." She turned and walked toward the moon, which hung like a spotlight in the heavens.

Tawny followed her aunt for what seemed an eternity before venturing the question, "What's next?"

"We're almost there. It's what I was looking for on the maps. I've been hearing cries since yesterday. It's got to be big."

They kept walking.

Cassandra stopped, and then took Tawny gently by the shoulder, pulling her close. "Do you hear them?"

Tawny shook her head and looked up into her aunt's face.

"You have to listen with your heart."

They stood, hand in hand, on the glassy frozen ripples.

A sad hum rose within Tawny's mind. She didn't hear it, yet she didn't imagine it. The sound was nothing like anything she had heard, or felt, before tonight.

Cassandra said, "Close your eyes. Take some deep breaths. Feel the moonlight on your face and think about the water churning below your feet."

Tawny's heartbeat quickened.

"Don't let your imagination scare you." Cassandra squeezed Tawny's hand. "Picture only what is, not what may happen.

Just feel the energy from the moon and the motion below us."

Cassandra raised her hands, lifting Tawny's.

Tawny kept her eyes shut. Pins and needles ran up and down her arms and legs, like electricity flowing through her muscles and skin.

The moon bridge shook, an earthquake upon the water, almost toppling Tawny, but Cassandra stiffened her arm and gripped her niece's hand to keep her steady.

Tawny started to speak, but the words caught in her throat.

A section of the bridge in front of them erupted, sending shards of solid water into the sky, where they glistened in the moonlight, quivered, and became strings of droplets raining upon the sea in a great deluge.

From the explosion rose a white fishing boat the size of a small house. Broken outrigger pieces held together by tangles of green fishing line dangled over the sides. Blue flakes of paint clung to the boards of a roofless wheelhouse. A gash in the boat's side explained the craft's demise.

"Did you do that?" Tawny gasped. "Did you just lift that boat up out of the water?"

"No. We did."

Tawny let go of her aunt's hand and took a few steps toward the dripping ghost from the deep. "I can hear them. It's like a hum, but I don't see anything."

Tawny took several big steps back and crossed her arms. "Are there any … any people on the boat?" Scenes from Funland's Haunted Mansion, only more real and gruesome, flashed in her mind.

"No, Tawny." Cassandra draped an arm across her niece's shoulder. "No people." She pulled a flashlight from her pack. "But this is when our work gets more dangerous. Shine your flashlight in front of your feet. Make sure you're stepping onto solid water with no cracks."

Tawny followed behind her aunt, stepping only where Cassandra had stepped.

"The sounds. The calls for help are getting louder," Tawny said.

They rounded the front of the boat and found a tangle of bright-green mesh draped in thick bunches over the side. The net bounced from the hull with slaps and thuds. Silver flashes within the net caught Tawny's eye.

"We have to work fast," said Cassandra. She stepped forward until her flashlight's beam danced on a liquid surface.

Cassandra placed her hands on her hips and bit her lip. "I can't reach the net."

Tawny said, "Give me your rope." She tied her flashlight to an end then tossed it. The flashlight passed through the net and tangled within the squirming mass.

"Great thinking, Tawny." Cassandra helped her niece pull the rope until they could reach the net and spread it on the moon bridge.

Fish by fish, they tossed each creature back into the ocean. The sound Tawny felt lessened with each splash but didn't go away completely.

"There are more up there." Cassandra pointed to a part of the net hanging over the boat's side. "We just can't reach them."

"Can't we make the water hard, like back with the turtle?"

"Not fast enough. Those fish have been out of the water too long, already. I'll have to climb the net."

"You're too heavy," Tawny said.

"Excuse me?"

Tawny took a deep breath. "Let me climb. I'm smaller."

Cassandra tied the rope around Tawny's waist. "If you tell your grandmother about this, we'll be sleeping in the shed for the rest of the summer."

"Don't let go of the rope, okay?"

"Never."

Tawny stepped to the hole's edge, clenched then unclenched her hands, knelt on the net, and began to crawl. The bunched mesh pressed into her palms. Pinched her fingers.

Tawny's foot slipped through the mesh. The net flipped upside-down, dangling her in the water. She screamed.

"Tawny," Cassandra yelled.

Tawny didn't stop screaming.

"Listen to me, Tawny."

Sobs replaced screams.

"Listen," Cassandra continued, "you're okay. I have you. You can do this. Kick your feet up into the net."

Tawny's feet brushed the tangled cordage but splashed back into the water, causing her grip to loosen.

"I'm falling!"

"Try again," Cassandra said.

Tawny swung her legs, hooking one foot into the net, then the other foot. "I did it!"

"I knew you could. Now, keep going."

Tawny found a bunch of shining and slippery spot fish, which she freed quickly, then started back toward the bridge.

A sudden feeling stopped her. It wasn't like the hum. This feeling thumped her hard, like a fist hitting her chest.

Tawny didn't like the thumping but felt drawn to it. She moved, hand over hand, to her left.

"Do you see something?" asked Cassandra.

Two jaws—rows of pointed saw-teeth gleaming white in the moonlight—thrust from between thick folds and snapped at Tawny's face. The massive creature, easily her size, twirled and writhed, jerking the net violently.

Tawny screamed and spun away.

"It's a shark." Cassandra walked back and forth along the hole's edge, working Tawny's safety rope, trying to keep it from tangling. "She's scared and can't breathe."

"*She's* scared?" yelled Tawny. "What about me?"

"You have to help her."

"How? She'll bite me."

"Climb down and around her tail. She can't move. Use your knife to cut the net from the bottom. Just stay away from her mouth."

Tawny pulled her knife from the zippered pocket on her sleeve.

"Stay to the shark's left and cut the net with your right hand so she doesn't slap you with her body. She doesn't want to hurt you, but she's scared."

Tawny moved slowly, not taking her eyes off the shark's head.

The net began to fall away from the silvery body until the shark slipped from between the net's folds and darted away.

Water lapping against the boat became the only sound.

Tawny hugged the plastic mesh, hanging, crying, and swinging gently.

"Great work, Tawny!"

Tawny nodded yet couldn't stop crying.

Cassandra looked at the moon and waited a few long moments before saying, "We can't leave the net, or the same thing will happen, again. You need to cut it free."

Hand over hand, Tawny climbed to the top of the net and scrambled over the boat's side. She cut the lines securing the net to the boat, and Cassandra pulled the tangled green mass onto the moon bridge.

"How am I going to get back?" Tawny asked.

"Now we can take our time and close the hole." Cassandra waved her hands over the water, hardening a path to the boat.

Tawny scanned the horizon. She had wanted to be like her aunt and had discovered that she was, in ways she never could have imagined.

Cassandra finished, helped Tawny down from the boat, and they gathered the net into a green mound.

"What do we do with it?" Tawny kicked the material with her boot.

"We can use the raft Riggs gave us." Cassandra pulled a pin from the metal cylinder and tossed the attached bundle of rubber tubing into the water.

Within minutes, they had piled the net into the small rubber craft, attached their rope to its nose, and begun to pull the load along the edge of the moon bridge to shore. The moment they stepped upon the sand, the bridge disappeared, and the boat sank back into the ocean's dark waters.

Tawny readjusted her school backpack, glancing again at the duct-tape repair she had made to the side pocket. She didn't want her lunch dropping out onto the road again.

She paused on the bridge and looked down into the stream to where she had once hidden among the rushes. The girls came behind her, and then passed, giggling and glancing over their shoulders at Tawny.

Tawny sensed their surprise when she caught up to them, said, "Hey, Susan, Allie, and Justina," and walked past them.

From behind, she heard the girls exchange comments, even heard her name, but she didn't stop and didn't care.

Dave Cooper is a history and martial arts teacher with almost twenty-five years of experience in each field. His first article appeared in The National Middle School Association's *Middle Ground* in 2003. Since then, he has contributed to a variety of periodicals including *Teaching History, Middle Level Learning, Family Chronicle, Boy's Life, College Bound*, and *Pennsylvania Educational Leadership*. His fiction and poetry have appeared in *Timber Creek Review, Yorick Magazine,* and *NFG*. Dave continues to teach and write in Lancaster, Pennsylvania. More of his work can be found at www.dcwriting.wordpress.com.

SAM SHADE, PRIVATE EYE

BY JACKSON COPPLEY

She looked like trouble. That, I could be sure of. Why, of all the joints, in all the towns, in all the world, did she have to choose my store in Rehoboth Beach?

The name's Sam Shade. It used to be something else, but the FBI changed it. Witness Protection Program. Seems some wise guys in Jersey didn't like what I had to say about them. So, the feds set me up here in this beach town in a new business, selling sunglasses. They chose the new business, the new identity, and the new name. Shade selling sunglasses? Seems someone at the bureau had a sense of humor.

Anyhow, back to the dame. She sauntered in to my shop one day in early May. It was a cool, cloudy day. Not much traffic in and out of the shop. She wore a red print sundress. Her long, brown hair hung below a beige straw hat, the soft type she could pull down over one eye. The dress came to her knees, showing off a set of gams that went from here to forever. She was so hot she could melt a box of Dolles taffy.

"Sam Shade?" she asked.

"That's right."

"Are you the same man that ran a private-eye agency in Jersey?"

"Maybe," I answered, realizing the G-men's attempt to hide

my past had more holes than cheap swiss cheese.

She played it cool, pulling out a cigarette and placing it between lips shimmering with fire-engine-red gloss. I reached for my Bic lighter and clicked it on before I realized she had a vape, not a cigarette. Should have known better. I have one myself, charging right there on the counter. Trying to cut back on my two-pack-a-day Camel habit. Seems my reflexes hadn't caught up to my new ways.

She grinned at my clumsy attempt and, glancing at my vape on the counter, said, "I just need a charge. Mind plugging me in?"

I didn't say anything about the other possible meanings, but her seductive smile said it all. I unplugged my vape and attached hers before taking the next step.

"So, what can I do for you, doll? You need a pair of sunglasses today?"

Her mood turned dark, as if a shadow had passed over her. "It's my husband," she said.

Yeah, a husband. Why was I not surprised? When you've been in the gumshoe business as long as me, you hear same old song sung by a new singer.

"I think he's having an affair."

"What makes you think that?" I asked.

"He's out late, telling me he's gone for a walk. He comes home with lipstick on his collar, smelling of cheap perfume."

"Well," I say, "he may have a good reason."

"It's happened ten times so far."

"Ten good reasons?" I reply lamely. "You know who it is?"

"It's my husband," she responded, perplexed.

"No, I mean who the woman is?" This lady may not be playing with a full deck.

"I think it's his secretary."

"His secretary?"

"Gesundheit."

"I didn't sneeze."

"No," she says. "His secretary's name is Gesundheit, Wilma Gesundheit."

"I see."

"What's your husband's name?"

"Gordon. Everyone calls him Gordy, Gordy N. Knott."

I realized this case would be harder to unravel than I expected.

"So, your name's Knott?" I asked.

"Not what?"

"Your name's the same as your husband's, Knott?"

"No, it's not."

"That's what I said," thinking, for some reason, of Abbott and Costello.

"No, my name is Windsor, Susan Windsor." I didn't take his name for an obvious reason.

"I get it." I laughed. "Windsor Knott."

"Huh?" she says, again with a clueless look. "No, his mother's name is Susan. We would have had the same name."

"But you still have the same first name. If someone yelled 'Susan' in a crowd ..." I realized I might reach closing hours at this rate. "You have a picture of your husband?"

"Sure thing," she said, as she reached in her purse and pulled out an iPhone. "I can do you one better. I've got a picture of the two of them together."

She flipped through some photos and came up with a shot.

"This was taken at his last office party."

I could see a dumpy little man looking into the camera, with a bleached blonde smiling it up, her face beside his, all snuggle-like. The woman had floozy written all over her.

"Can I have a copy?"

"Sure, want me to AirDrop it to your phone? Or I can Facebook Messenger it. How about I send it in a message?"

I had to stop her as I silently cursed. What ever happened to a printed photo?

"Look," I tell her. "Just send it in an email. Can you do that?"

"Sure."

I handed her my business card. "There's just one thing I want to know."

"What's that?"

"What do you want me to do? I mean you could just ask your husband, right?"

"No, I can't do that."

"Why not?"

"He's disappeared."

If you're going to hunt down a missing husband, there's only one place to look in Rehoboth—Whiskey Jack's. That much I'd learned since the feds made this town my home. Chuck, the bartender, knows the scoop on everyone, because sooner or later he's wiping the bar in front of them.

Whiskey Jack's reminded me of my old watering hole in Jersey. But you'd have to clean up the regulars and put flip-flops on their feet. I wondered whether the Jersey crowd boasted as many tattoos as the folks here. The other thing different? In Rehoboth, there's an ocean across the boardwalk and no wall to obstruct the view. Nice.

Chuck was on duty. Seems he always was, or at least he was when I came around. I took a seat, but before I could catch Chuck's eye, this young blonde, all bouncy and bright-eyed, comes over and asks, "What can I get for you?"

"Beer," I say.

"What kind? We have Bud, Bud Light, Coors, Coors Light, Corona, Corona Light …"

She's looking off into nowhere reciting this list. I try to interrupt, but I can't squeeze a word in edgewise.

"Heineken, Keystone, Stella Arto, uh Artist, Artois… I never can say that one right," she smiles, but goes on.

All the while I'm listening ("Yuengling, Yuengling Light …"), I'm thinking of those flicks where a guy like me goes into a bar and orders just "beer," and the bartender asks no questions and pours him something. What's the something, I wonder?

The blonde finally gets to the end of her list and I ask, "Do you have Miller High Life?"

I like the classics.

I can see her running through the list she just gave me in her head as she clicks off each with her thumb and forefinger until she gets to what I just asked for.

"Sure thing. Coming right up," she says, and dashes off.

This is my chance to get Chuck's attention. He comes over.

"Well, look who the cat drug in," he says.

Chuck's an old salt. Don't know if he was ever a sailor, but he looked the part. Middle-aged, squat, with a grizzled face always in need of a shave. If he had a peg leg, he could ace a part in *Moby Dick*.

"How're you doing?" I asked.

"Can't complain. It ain't going to change the world if I did."

I had to snicker. You see, Chuck and me had had this back and forth a dozen times, and each time, he had a new answer to "How're you doing?":

"Can't complain. Not going to lower the rent."

"Can't complain. Not going to win me the lottery."

"Can't complain. You're still going to come around."

I liked that last one the best.

"Look, Chuck," I said, pulling up my cell phone and holding up a picture.

"Who's the dumpy guy?" Chuck asked.

"His name's Knott."

"Not what?"

"No, it's *K, N, O, T, T*. Knott. Gordy N. Knott."

"Who's the dame?"

"Gesundheit."

"I didn't sneeze."

"Believe it or not, that's her name."

"Gesundheit?"

"Yep. Wilma Gesundheit."

"Sam, I didn't know her name, but, sure, I know the dame. She's a regular."

"Is that so?"

"See that stool over there?" he said, pointing to a lonely spot at the corner of the bar.

"Yeah."

"The lady comes every day and sits herself there."

"And when does she do this?"

"4 p.m. on the dot."

I decide then and there I might need another beer that afternoon at four.

I closed the shop early and took a stroll to the boardwalk. The usual crowd of tired, sunbaked day-trippers dragged their whining broods along. I'm not much on kids. Guess it's good no female trapped this flatfoot.

It didn't take long to reach Whiskey Jack's. Sure enough, 4 p.m. and Miss Floozy sat in her usual spot, sipping something pink. She glanced my way with a come-hither look that made me think twice. It was a well-practiced look, the type a woman like her had in a bag full of tricks.

The stool beside her was empty, so I slid into it. Miss bouncy blonde waitress walked up to me. I said, "A beer," and before she started her list, I corrected the order and said, "Miller High Life."

"Draft or bottle?"

"Jeez," I thought, "Why didn't I get that choice earlier?"

"Bottle."

Miss Bouncy was about to ask me another question. Probably the size of the bottle. I didn't know, or care. A steely stare from me sent her on her way. Turning to the woman beside me, I asked, "Come here often?"

"Ya know, I come here every day. Why haven't I seen you before?"

She said all this in a high-pitched, nasal whine that put her back in the floozy category. But I pushed on.

"Just lucky, I guess." I put out my hand. "Shade's the name. Sam Shade."

"How do you do," she said, taking my hand. Her hand was soft as a baby's behind. Probably hadn't ever lifted anything heavier than an eyebrow pencil. "My name is Wilma, Wilma Gesundheit."

I didn't say anything about her name. "Wilma, I'm wondering something."

"What's that?"

"I'm wondering if you know somebody by the name of Gordy Knott?"

"Say, what is this?" she said, her over-manicured claws coming out.

"Look," I said. "I'd love to chit-chat and get to know you,

but this story has a word-count limit and I can't beat around the bush. Knott's wife hired me. He's missing."

"Missing? Gordy? That can't be."

"Why not?"

"'Cause I love the big lug."

I stayed mum. The lady was on a roll.

"Gordy is a gentleman. You know what I mean? He didn't even make fun of my name."

"I guess it was bad as a kid, huh?"

"Bad? Every day, the girls would sing the Flintstones song when they laid eyes on me."

"Huh?" I said. Seems this story was going somewhere I didn't expect.

"You know, 'Flintstones. Meet the Flintstones. They're the modern stone-age family.'"

"Yeah, yeah. I know the song."

She was almost in tears. "Wilma is an awful name. Wilma Flintstone is all the kids could think of."

"I see," I said. Didn't the kids she knew ever sneeze?

"Ya see, Gordy was the only guy who got it. He didn't ever call me Wilma."

"What did he call you?"

"He called me by my middle name."

"What's that?"

"Betty."

Was it just me, or was everyone in this town nuts?

"He loved me, see? He was going to leave his wife."

"That so?"

"I saw him just yesterday. Later, he dropped a note off for me at my apartment. Guess he was in a hurry."

"What did it say?"

"I don't know."

"You don't know?" I was thinking this dame was both nuts and illiterate.

"I mean I don't know what it means."

"You got the note on you?"

"Sure," she said, opening a bag large enough to hold supplies for a ten-day camping trip. She started digging. "I know it's here somewhere."

After putting a fist-sized set keys on the bar, along with two types of headache relief, a makeup kit, a mirror, and a feminine product I would have rather not have seen, she came up with an envelope.

"There!" she beamed, handing me a beige envelope embossed with the initials GNK.

I opened the note. Scrawled across the note was "Meet me. BPH 203."

"See," she said. "I don't know what it means."

"I do," I replied.

I figured a guy like Gordy, with a woman on the side, was no stranger to hotels. So, it made sense that BPH was the Boardwalk Plaza Hotel and 203 was the room number. I have a sixth sense, and it's not about seeing dead people. It's about trouble, and I knew there was trouble in Room 203. So, I called up Windsor to meet me there. She didn't know I would be bringing Wilma and another special guest.

I arrived first and spent some quality time in the lobby talking to the bird. People don't know this hotel by its formal name. They know it as "the pink hotel" due to the color on the outside. The inside is all quaint-like, with antiques everywhere and a parrot in a cage. I was telling the parrot he should meet my friend Chuck. I could see him on Chuck's shoulder, headed to Treasure Island.

Just as the parrot squawked its agreement, in sashays Windsor, gorgeous as ever in another red sundress. She's not looking as relaxed as the first time I saw her.

"Got your message," she said. "Why are we here?"

Before I could answer, the other member of our little party came through the door. Wilma had changed into a red sundress that looked just like the one Windsor wore. I expected a not-too-happy encounter between these two, but the fashion faux pas poured gas on the fire.

"You!" shouted Windsor. "What's she doing here?"

Wilma had a similar question for me. "Say, what's the big idea?"

"Ladies," I said. "I want to take a little trip up to Room 203."

I watched for reactions from the two and could read each like a book.

"But first, I want you to meet a friend of mine."

A trim young man wearing the green and black uniform of Rehoboth's finest stepped into view.

"I'd like you to meet Officer Miranda from the Rehoboth police."

"Ladies," said the officer.

I could see the two going through a list of transgressions in their heads, and I don't mean traffic tickets.

"Let's head up to Room 203," I said, and walked to the elevator.

We gathered outside the door as Miranda used a pass key to open it. We stepped in, and both women gasped.

Sprawled on the carpet was Mr. Gordon N. Knott, or should I say the late Gordy Knott? The dumpy little guy lay on his back with a wide-eyed expression frozen on his puss. Something was shoved deep into his big mouth. On closer examination, I could see that the something was a cotton-candy cone, still containing bits of the blue confection.

"You killed my husband!" yelled Windsor at Wilma.

Wilma stood there, sniffling. "I did not!"

"So, you confess?" asked Miranda.

"What?" asked the confused Wilma.

"You said you did Knott."

I stepped in. "No, Miranda. She was denying it. Although, it was true that she was doing Knott."

Now, it was Miranda's turn to looked confused.

"Not so fast, sweetheart," I said to Windsor. "You're missing a few details."

As I spoke, Wilma seemed to be losing it. Miranda handed her a handkerchief, into which she blew hard.

"Something about that note her husband wrote looked fishy. I took it and looked at the writing on the check Windsor gave me. I'm no expert, but I bet if I gave them to one, he'd tell me the same person wrote both."

"Her husband wrote you a check?" asked Miranda.

After I rolled my eyes, I continued.

"Something else about that note. It smelled like cotton candy."

"I hate cotton candy," said Wilma. "I'm allergic to the stuff."

"That's probably why you're sniffling, gorgeous. This place reeks of it."

Windsor looked cagey, like a cornered animal.

"That day you came into my shop, your perfume couldn't cover something else I smelled. I couldn't figure it out then, but I know now. Cotton candy."

"So, who killed him?" asked Miranda.

Wilma sneezed.

"Gesundheit," said Miranda.

"Huh?" said Wilma.

"No," I said. "Susan Windsor."

Windsor unraveled.

"You don't know what it was like. He was always cheating. Comes home with my favorite, cotton candy. Sure, some girls get roses, but he knew my weakness. I love the stuff. The only reason I moved here. But when he came home with cotton candy, I knew he was up to no good. Plus ..."

"Yeah?" I said. "Go on."

"He was cheating so much, and all the cotton candy was making me fat. I had to take drastic action."

"Like choking the guy on the stuff?"

"That or join Weight Watchers."

Made sense.

"He wanted to make up. Had me come here to this room. Of course, he had a cone of the gooey stuff. I ate it up. That is, until he said he wanted a divorce. He told me he'd met the love of his life."

Between sniffles, Wilma uttered a girly "Aww ..."

After shooting a look her way that could kill, Windsor stepped up and latched onto me, pleading with her baby blues full of tears. "You see, Sam, don't ya? I had no choice. No jury would convict me."

"We'll have to see about that, sweetheart," I said. "Just one thing left to do. Miranda?"

The officer walked up as I pushed her away.

"Read Windsor her rights, Miranda."

I went to Gordy's funeral. One of the few times I had to wear a tie. Putting it on reminded me of Windsor. She's in the federal pen nearby. Maybe, I'll give her a visit someday.

Wilma Gesundheit is in therapy for her cotton candy allergy. She tells me her therapist and receptionist are nice, always calling out her name.

The season came to an end. I close the shop early most days. And I take the time to wander the boardwalk after sunset and think. Guess where I landed isn't so bad after all. I sell a few sunglasses and handle a few cases here and there. Just like the old days. Someone always has a few loose ends they need Sam Shade to tie up.

Jackson Coppley is the author of *Leaving Lisa*, and *The Code Hunters: A Nicholas Foxe Adventure*. His short stories appear in *Tales From Our Near Future, Beach Life, Bay to Ocean*, and other publications. He writes a daily blog on his website, www.JacksonCoppley.com. The blog entry, *Steve Jobs and Me,* won an award from Delaware Press Association. A graduate in physics, Coppley's resume includes a career with world communications and technology companies and the launching of what the press called "a revolutionary software program." Now a full-time writer, his work focuses on adventure, but *Sam Shade* reflects his humorous side. Coppley and his wife, Ellen, divide their time between homes in Rehoboth Beach, Delaware, and Chevy Chase, Maryland.

SUMMER OF THE GODS

BY JACOB JONES-GOLDSTEIN

The screen door slammed behind me as I ran out of the house. It was drizzling, and the grass on the lawn was slick enough that I almost lost my footing on the way to my bike. I heard my grandfather's ragged baritone boom behind me, "Don't let me catch you in this house during the day again!"

I resisted the urge to flip him off as I pedaled out into the street and toward town. The rainwater thankfully hid the tears streaming down my face. It was going to be another long and miserable summer.

Downtown Rehoboth was a few miles from the house. By the time I got there, I had calmed down some. It was a Friday, and still early in the morning, so not much was open. The rain had let up, but it was starting to look as though the worst was yet to come, and the prospects for me finding a place to get out of the rain were grim. During previous summers, I'd learned that most of the cafes and coffee shops didn't want a kid hanging around for hours on his own. I'd spent yesterday wasting time in the souvenir stores, so if I did that again they would probably chase me out. My dad had given me a couple of bucks, so I could kill the afternoon at Funland, but that didn't open till one.

On a whim, I turned down Columbia. It was the longest, straightest street in town, which made it fun to race up and down. I rode along the street a ways and was about to start trying to break land-speed records when I saw a shop I'd never noticed before.

It was a one-story place next to a small rundown house with a large old oak tree. The shop looked a little ramshackle, too. The roof sagged, and the posters in the windows had yellowed in the sun. An awning ran the length of the building, with a couple of inviting benches underneath. Above the awning was a hand-stenciled sign that read "Beans Records." A sign on the door announced that the store was open, which was all the invitation I needed. I parked my bike and went inside.

A little bell above the door chimed as I walked through. The store was as shambolic on the inside as it was on the outside. Racks of records, eight-tracks, and cassettes were everywhere. Crates filled with vinyl albums covered the floor. A rusty spinner overflowed with sheet music. To the left of the entrance was a counter and on the far side of the room was what looked like a phone booth. The store smelled musty, but not in a bad way—more like the way you'd imagine Bob Dylan smelled in 1965. I didn't recognize the song playing, but I kind of liked it.

"Good morning! You're up early on this rainy and miserable day," a jovial voice said. It surprised me enough that I gave a little start. I had not seen anyone when I first looked around. He was standing in one of the aisles, leaning on a stack of records.

"Uh … hi," I said. My witty conversational style is one of the reasons I don't have a lot of friends.

The man stood around 5' 9". I was tall and gawky for my age, so he wasn't much taller than me, but he was stocky, with shaggy black hair and a beard that was trimmed but looked like he'd done the trimming with a pair of safety scissors. His T-shirt read "Keep on Truckin'."

"Can I help you find anyth— Oh, it's you!" he exclaimed.

"Uh …" I managed to croak, confused. I had barely spoken in a day or two. My dad hadn't had much to say since we got here, and my speaking seemed to anger my grandfather no matter what I said, so I kept quiet most of the time.

He laughed in a friendly way and looked me over, tapping his lip with his index finger and furrowing his brow.

It made me a little uncomfortable to be scrutinized. "What do you mean it's—"

"One moment," he said, cutting me off. "I've almost got it."

"Got what?"

"Aha! I know just the thing."

He walked down the aisle, stopping in a section marked "L." He flipped through some of the records and pulled one out. He held it up like a minister presenting a newly baptized baby to the congregation.

"You look like you need to learn the basics before exploring on your own," he said, motioning wildly to the rest of the store. "Take this home, listen to it at least twice, then come back tomorrow." He handed me the record.

"I don't think I have enough to pay for—"

He cut me off with a wave of his hand, "It's yours. A gift. Take it. Come back tomorrow. We'll do introductions then."

He walked over to the counter and reached behind it, pulling out a plastic bag. "You'll need this; it's going to pour." He had a way of moving and gesturing that felt flamboyant but utterly nonthreatening.

"Okay, out you go. I have a busy day and you have work to do."

"But—"

"No buts. Come back tomorrow."

He all but pushed me out the door. I turned around to ask a question, and he shut the door in my face. He flipped the open sign to closed, waved through the window, and locked the door before disappearing into the back of the store.

For a long time, I stood looking at the closed sign, wondering what had just happened. Eventually, there was a crack of thunder and the rain began pouring down.

I made it to Rehoboth Avenue, and went in one of the emptier-looking coffee shops. I hoped that, with the rain, they might cut me some slack before kicking me out. I bought a hot chocolate, settled into one of the big fluffy armchairs, and took the record out of the bag.

I had never owned a record. My dad didn't listen to much besides the news and the occasional ballgame. I wondered if he'd stopped listening to music when my mom died, like he stopped doing so many other things. I don't remember much music in our house, even before she passed away.

The cover of the record he had given me had a blimp bursting into flames in black and white, and the words "Led Zeppelin." Four weird-looking dudes stared at me from the back cover, surrounding a list of songs. I traced my finger down the tracks, quietly reading the names of each out loud. I'd heard of the band, and maybe seen people wearing T-shirts for them, but I had no idea what to expect or why he'd given me this particular album.

"Hey, kid, you want to put that on?" said the long-haired young woman who had made my hot chocolate.

I looked around in confusion before realizing I was the only one in the shop.

"Yes, you," she said, laughing.

"Uh, sure," I managed. This made two people I'd talked to today. It was shaping up to be a banner day on my social calendar.

I walked over and handed her the record.

"Led Zeppelin. Nice! Shame it's not their fourth," she said after looking it over. She stripped off the plastic wrap and slid the vinyl circle out of the sleeve. There was a record player behind the counter playing a song I didn't recognize. She picked the arm up and the music cut out while the disc slowly came to a halt. I held my breath as she switched records.

After a quick look around to see if anyone was about to come in, she winked at me, and turned the volume up.

As the first guitar notes blared out of the speakers, my pupils dilated, my heartbeat synced up with the drumbeat, and I knew I would never be the same.

When I got home that night, I asked my dad if there was a record player I could use. He disappeared into the basement and returned with a turntable that had a built-in speaker and a pair of headphones. His melancholy look made me wonder what memories it held.

I took the record player and headed upstairs to play my record, thinking only of listening to that incredible music all night. I got to the top of the stairs and turned down the hall.

My grandfather.

He stood at the end of the hall glaring at me, and then slowly began to walk toward me. He usually towered over me, but his time he bent down on one knee and looked me in the eye. He cleared his throat and said in a menacing whisper, "If I hear one note from that, I'm going to break your record and then you, in that order."

I said nothing, trying to not breathe.

Slowly, he got up from his knee, straightened his pants, and walked down the stairs. I swallowed hard and walked to my room.

Taking no chances, I closed the door to my room, took the covers off the bed, and stuffed them under the door. I made sure to attach the headset before even plugging in the player. Once that was done, I sat cross-legged in front of the turntable, laid the record on the mat, put the headphones on, and gently dropped the needle. The guitar washed over me and pushed thoughts of my grandfather out of my head.

The next day, I left as early as possible to avoid any more trouble. The rain had stopped overnight, and the sun was cooking off the dampness, making the streets misty. I imagined the mist as dry ice, rising off the stage as Led Zeppelin tore through "Communication Breakdown." I was so lost in the fantasy, I shot through an intersection and heard tires screech behind me, followed by yelling. I didn't look back. The music had me feeling invincible.

I pulled up to the store expecting to have to wait, but the open sign was out, and the light was on, so I went on in.

"Well, hello again," said the man who had given me the record yesterday. "I trust you did your homework?"

I wanted to show my gratitude and express everything the album had made me think and feel, but I had no idea how.

"It was amazing," I nearly shouted. "Thank you so, so, so much for it."

"Well, for that, I am truly glad," he said happily. "Let's take a look at what we have for you today, shall we, Jesse?"

I stared at him. I couldn't remember telling him my name.

"My name is Beans, by the by. We need to work a little on your loquaciousness. Hard to get a word in edgewise."

"How'd you know my name?"

"It's a small town. I know most everyone. I knew your dad years ago."

"Really?" I was shocked. I couldn't imagine my father buying records.

"Yep. He was quite the music aficionado. I know your grandfather, too."

"Oh," I responded anxiously.

"Not to worry. I wouldn't attribute any of your grandfather's personality to you." He had an odd, sing-song way of talking.

"Uh … thanks."

"Uh … you're welcome," he said, jokingly. "So, for today, I think we shall assign you this." He handed me a record with a bunch of old-timey people on it. At the top it said, "Led Zeppelin II."

"Thank you, but I still can't pay."

"Fear not. You can't put a price on education."

"The lady at the cafe mentioned Led Zeppelin IV?"

Beans laughed. "One shouldn't skip ahead."

"Uh, okay. May I ask how you know my grandfather?"

"You certainly may. I might even be inclined to answer. Come outside."

He grabbed a pipe off the counter and walked out. I followed.

I watched as he packed the pipe full of sweet-smelling tobacco, lit it, and took a deep puff.

"It's nice outside on these mornings, before all the people descend on our little town," he said wistfully. "Your grandfather is a miserable old bastard who revels in making life hard on everyone he encounters. No one has ever been happy to run into him. For years he has been a dark cloud over this town."

I stared wide-eyed at him. I had always been told to be polite and respectful to everyone, but especially the elderly. I knew deep down I hated my grandfather, but I could never articulate that, because respecting my elders was so ingrained. To hear someone say it out loud was shocking.

"Alas, we don't choose our families, and even in a town as nice as this, we can't always choose our neighbors."

He smiled and puffed on his pipe for a while. I stood quietly with him, watching the clouds of smoke drift away.

After he finished his pipe and tapped the ashes out, he smiled and said, "You should be running along. If you go to the cafe again, tell Kate that she should appreciate the rest of

Zeppelin more. She's always in a hurry. Come back tomorrow, and we'll see about Zeppelin III."

I went to the cafe and told the woman I now knew to be Kate what Beans had said. She laughed and put my new record on. I was mesmerized. After it was done, I asked Kate about Beans.

"He's been here at least as long as I have. His store is always open when I stop by, but I never see anyone else in there. I asked him once about his name. He said that it was a childhood nickname based on that little song, you know, 'beans, beans, the musical fruit'? That's about all I know."

Kate had to take the record off when other customers came in. I had planned to go to Funland, but now all I wanted to do was go home and listen to the music. My whole world had shrunk down to a couple of wax discs filled with magic, mystery, and guitars.

That night, I meant to ask my dad about Beans and listening to music, but he was more distant than usual, so I didn't bother. I went up to my room after dinner and fell asleep with my headphones on.

Beans was waiting for me with Led Zeppelin III when I arrived at the store early the next morning. He told me to go to the library and check out *The Fellowship of the Ring*. He said some of the lyrics would make more sense to me if I read it.

I dutifully marched down to the library and checked out the book. My reading was mostly confined to *Mad* magazines and comic books. I'd read a couple of books for school, but my interest in the likes of *Johnny Tremain* and *Where the Red Fern Grows* was limited.

I spent the rest of the day in Kate's coffee shop. She told

me any friend of Beans was a friend of hers and I could stay as long as I liked.

Kate and I listened to the record together; I was blown away. It was different from the other two, and there was something mystical about it that I couldn't quite wrap my head around. I assumed that was why Beans had told me to read the book. I drank hot cocoa and read about hobbits until it was closing time. It was the happiest day I could ever remember having.

Monday morning started off poorly. The coffee shop was closed, and as I rode to the store, the clouds were darkening apocalyptically. The weather report called for a huge storm and possible flooding. I couldn't wait to listen to Led Zeppelin IV but had nowhere to go but the house, and that meant risking the wrath of my grandfather.

My hopes to hang out at the store were dashed when I arrived and found the place dark and a "closed" sign on the door. I thought he might just be closed to the general public, so I parked my bike and went over to check the door. It was locked, but there was a bag leaning against it with my name on it. My heart leapt. Inside the bag was a copy of Led Zeppelin IV with a note on it that read:

Dearest Jesse,

I have some errands to run today, but I should be back later if you'd like to come by. In the meantime, please enjoy this record. It was your dad's favorite.

Beans

I admired the album cover for a few minutes. The bent old man in the picture could have been Beans. The resemblance was uncanny.

As I stood there, entranced, there was a huge crack of thunder. I looked up and saw that the sky had turned a menacing shade of green and it looked like it was getting ready to pour. I had a decision to make: go home and hope my grandfather would let me in, or try and find a place to hole up in town.

A flash of lightning with a thunderclap following closely after made the decision for me. I hopped on my bike and raced home. It started raining three quarters of the way there, and really started coming down as I got to the driveway. My dad's car wasn't there, and I hoped my grandfather had gone with him. I jumped off my bike, letting it slide to a halt on the front yard, and ran for the door.

I made it into the house just as the deluge began. Standing in the foyer, dripping wet and trying to catch my breath, I heard my grandfather bellow.

"What did I tell you about being in this house during the day?"

His yell was followed by a staccato burst of thunder.

"Sorry, Grandpa. It's just that everything was closed and it's raining really hard."

I heard the creak of his armchair as he got up. I was paralyzed with fear and didn't know what to do, so I just stood there dripping.

He entered the foyer and glared at me for what felt like an hour. Eventually, he said in a low and menacing voice, "Clean up that water and go to your room. I don't want to hear a SOUND from you. Your father will be home later, and we will talk about places for you to be during the day when it rains." He sneered while saying "rains."

While he went back to his chair, I mopped up the water and then bolted upstairs, closing the door to my room and breathing a sigh of relief. It took a while to calm down and stop shaking. I unwrapped my new record as quietly as I could. Reverently, I placed it on the turntable, slipped the headphones over my ears, turned up the volume, and dropped the needle.

There was a crackle or two, a sound like an engine starting, and then Robert Plant shouted "Hey hey mama said the way you move, gon' make you sweat, gon' make you groove," followed by a burst of guitars and drums.

I let the music pour over me and wash away the fear and anger I felt at my grandfather. Each song was like a magic spell cast over me, chipping away at my childhood and leaving me older in its wake. Lightning flashed and thunder crashed while I listened, and I imagined I could almost feel hair begin to grow on my chest.

"When the Levee Breaks" came on and I couldn't sit still anymore. I turned the volume up to 10, stood up, and began to play air guitar and drums. I imagined the lightning was illuminating the sky in time with the music. The rain pounding the roof was in tune with Page's guitar. The thunder sounded with John Bonham's cymbals. It was rock and roll ecstasy.

And then I tripped backward over my suitcase.

I slammed to the floor, yanking the headphones out of the record player. The volume was all the way up and music began to blare shockingly loudly. I recovered and dove at the machine to turn it off. As soon as I did, I heard a crash from downstairs and my grandfather screamed, "That's it."

I scrambled to my feet as I heard him charging up the stairs.

I had no idea he could move that fast.

I stood frozen as he kicked the door open.

"What did I tell you?" he said, in an almost calm way, despite the rage I could see in his face.

I started to speak but he told me to shut up.

He walked over to the player, picked up the record, and snapped it in half.

"No!"

He spun on me and said, "What did you say to me?" He was grinning when he said it, like I had just given him all the excuse he needed.

"Why are you such an asshole?" I shouted. The broken record, that moments ago meant everything to me, was still in his hands, making me furious.

I didn't even see his hand as it flashed out and struck me across the face. I don't know if there was a lightning bolt or if the white light I saw was from pain as I screamed and hit the floor.

"I'm going to teach you some manners, just like I had to teach your father." He lifted his foot and kicked me in the stomach. As I doubled over, he paused and cracked the knuckles on the hand he'd hit me with.

I had two options: curl into a ball and let him beat me or get out of there. I chose the latter. I kicked out at his foot, which surprised him and caused him to stumble backwards. That gave me my chance.

I rushed down the stairs and out the front door. The rain was coming down so hard I could barely see the street, but my grandfather was right behind me, so I ran toward where I'd dropped my bike.

"Get back here," he screamed.

I hopped on the bike and tore down the street, pedaling as fast as I could. The only place I could think to go was Beans's store.

I heard a car behind me, the horn honking wildly. My grandfather was following me. I don't know how I kept ahead of him in the rain. I took every turn at the last second, rode across yards and through alleys. I was sure he meant to kill me.

Somehow, I made it to the store without him running me over. I was overwhelmed with relief when I saw the light on. My grandfather wasn't far behind, but I knew Beans would protect me. I rode the bike onto the lawn and fell over in the wet grass. Scrambling to the door, I ripped it open, and dove into the store.

My grandfather's car stopped in the street. He emerged from the driver's side, walked to where I had dumped my bike, and stopped. He looked around and shouted, "Where did you go, you little bastard?"

I took a step back from the door in confusion.

"He can't see us," a voice behind me said calmly.

Outside, my grandfather continued to shout threats. He kicked my bike in fury.

"This place isn't for everyone," Beans said, as he handed me a towel. "It's for special people who have a little magic in them. All he has is hate and spite."

"But ..." I started, but couldn't finish. Nothing made sense.

Softly, Beans said "You might want to close your eyes for this next part."

"When I find you, there's going to be hell—" he shouted, before he was cut off by a blinding light and blast of thunder. There was another crack a second later that wasn't thunder.

My grandfather turned around and threw his arms up as the oak tree that had just been struck by lightning landed on him.

"When the levee breaks, mama, you got to move," Beans said, putting his hand on my shoulder.

It was a week before I got to back to his store. My father dropped me off on the way back from the funeral. Beans was sitting on the bench in the sun, smoking his pipe. He watched as we unloaded my bike.

"Mr. Beans doesn't look like he's aged a day," my father said as he waved. "Don't be too late getting home. I'll make us some hamburgers for dinner."

"Sounds great, Dad."

I had a million questions about that night, but in the end, I decided to leave well enough alone. I doubt Beans would have answered any of them anyway.

"Great to see you again, Jesse, and don't you look sharp in your fancy suit. Why don't you come inside and we'll see what we have for you today. Perhaps you're ready for The Who."

I followed him into the store. The music playing wasn't something I recognized, but the lyrics I heard made me smile: "It's a town full of losers. I'm pulling out of here to win."

Jacob Jones-Goldstein is a fiction writer and sports journalist. His short stories have appeared both in the United States and abroad. Mostly focusing on the horror genre, he dabbles in magical realism and fantasy. Jacob covers professional sports for a Philadelphia regional news site, TapInto.Net, including a weekly column about the 76ers, "Winning Culture." He also writes about music for ShoutingStreet.com. Jacob lives in Delaware with his wife, a variety of cats, and possibly a ghost or two.

THE HOUSE THAT WOULDN'T BE SOLD

BY NANCY POWICHROSKI SHERMAN

Some people swear they're not afraid of living alone. Some swear they don't believe in ghosts. And some say, "Bah, humbug," to any claim of spirit visitation. Penny was one of those. But, then, she'd never actually experienced a real haunting—not until her search for a budget-friendly house took her to one considered unsellable.

Having recently graduated from college on full scholarship, Penny's parents had gifted her, as a graduation present, the money from a substantial college fund they had set up for her when she was born. It was the perfect opportunity to purchase a house before she wasted that money foolishly. She had always dreamed of living in Cape May, NJ, though she expected it would be difficult to find a house there within her means. Still, she had to at least try. Her new job as a web designer for a major marketing company would surely take care of monthly bills with some left over for the social life she expected to enjoy in a beach community.

The real estate agent, Sherry Allen, mentioned a great buy in Cape May just blocks from the ocean—on the market for over a decade, so the sellers were "motivated." And, if that one didn't fit her needs, then there were other older houses that "just needed a little TLC."

Penny had already assumed that any house within her budget would be an old house, probably one that needed work. She accepted that any such house would have squeaking floorboards and clanging pipes. Perhaps even the sound of bats in the attic or mice in the cellar. Her fearless attitude about living amid these noises informed her that such oddities would not be a problem. Unlike others who might be scared, she had never awoken from a nightmare with any belief that someone or something was in the house and coming to get her.

The morning after her contact with Beachside Real Estate, Penny drove to the house to meet Sherry. The front yard of the property was small—not unusual for downtown Cape May—but had a well-kept lawn. A walkway of smooth lapis-colored ceramic tiles led up to the front porch of the white cottage with navy shutters. The roof over the porch was held up by classic round pillars, but the absence of outdoor furniture was evidence that no one was living in the house.

She gathered her shoulder-length ginger hair into a scrunchy to cool off in the hot sun and sat on the top step to wait for the agent.

Sherry Allen arrived like a cyclone—sudden and highly energized. She leapt from the seat of her MINI Cooper Convertible, pushed her sunglasses up onto her short platinum hair, and strode to the porch. The agent's first words were, "This is the best deal. The current owners restored it to its pre-nineteenth-century style, with a dash of beach chic, while adding modern comforts like central air, updated plumbing and electric, wiring for Wi-Fi and cable television, and high-end appliances. Oh, and it comes fully furnished."

"So why has it been on the market for so long?" Penny asked.

The woman shrugged and affected a smile. "At first, the price was too high. Then, it was on the market too long." She handed a key to Penny. "I have to check on another property. Why don't you look around on your own? I'll be back in an hour to hear your comments and discuss an offer."

Before Penny could blink her eyes, Sherry was in her MINI and heading off.

Okay, that was strange, she thought, and speculated that maybe the house was still on the market because the agent wasn't very attentive.

As she put the key into the lock, she heard soft laughter coming from within the enclosed porch of the house next door, but its tarnished screens prevented her from seeing who was laughing. "Hi," Penny called out. "I might be your new neighbor."

The laugh again. Then a tiny voice replied, "Are you sure you want to live there?"

"Why wouldn't I?"

"Your real estate agent didn't go into the cottage with you. Did you wonder why?"

"I guess my agent is so successful and shows so many properties that she doesn't have time to provide a walking tour through every one of them." She couldn't believe she was defending Sherry Allen when she herself had thought the agent's quick exodus was strange.

"Did she share the story of The Wolfhound house?"

"Wolfhound?"

"That's what it's called."

"Why?"

The laughter again. "Maybe as a guardian to protect against spirits of the dead."

Although Penny had always rolled her eyes over warnings about ghosts, zombies, and other mysterious beings, those words sent an unexpected chill up her back. "Are you trying to scare me?"

"Just a warning. If you go inside to look around, don't be surprised by what you see or hear."

Was it curiosity or a tinge of hesitation Penny was feeling? "Did one of the previous owners die in this cottage?"

"Not recently. Well before I was born. And that was a long time ago."

Penny refused to believe that she was standing in front of what this neighbor claimed was a haunted house. "Obviously, since this house was built centuries ago, the chances are good that, in such early times, someone would have died in the house. It wasn't uncommon." She kept trying to see through the weathered screens that surrounded the neighbor's porch. She wanted to see the face that owned such a tiny voice. At first, she had thought she was talking with a child, but the words, *And that was a long time ago*, belied that. Maybe the neighbor just had a child-like voice.

"Who are you?" Penny asked.

"Just an old lady who has lived here all her life." The laughter that followed was interrupted by a hacking cough and the kind of wheezing associated with emphysema. This was definitely not a child playing a game.

Penny heard the door to the woman's house squeak open.

"Sometimes, a bit of knowing can save us from danger," the woman said. Then the door slammed shut. The woman had left the porch.

Well, that was odd. She's probably just trying to scare me. Maybe she likes the quiet of an empty house next to hers. Or maybe she's crazy, and that's why this "wolfhound house" isn't selling. I'm not going to allow some old lady to frighten me with silly warnings. Dead people? Really? Like in that Sixth Sense *movie?* Just to be sure, Penny felt her pulse. *Not dead.*

Once again, she put the key into the lock. She felt it turn so easily that she questioned whether it had moved on its own. *Don't let that woman get into your head.*

She shrugged it off when she opened the door and saw the interior of the great room. Not exactly open-concept, but a recent attempt at creating one. The walls that would have separated the vestibule and center hallway from the two side rooms had been removed, so the living room to the right and dining room to the left were now one spacious area. The original wide-plank floors had been refinished with a dark stain. The furnishings were professionally staged with beach-inspired details, and the shiplap walls were painted a medium blue.

It was all so beautiful. But something was wrong. Penny felt it throughout every inch of her body. *It's that old lady's fault. She put the suggestion of peril into my mind.*

Penny thought she heard the woman's peculiar laugh again, but that wasn't possible. The windows were closed and the air conditioning running. *It's only my imagination. I've never been scared of spirits that walk at night, or in this case, at morning.*

She shook off the feeling and focused on the central staircase leading to the second floor. It was certainly not the original. Its steps were wider at the bottom, followed by slightly decreasing widths above. A curving handrail was made of cherry wood with wrought-iron supports shaped like sea grass—an odd mix of regal old-world feeling and modern chic beach house. It was as though the owners had forced elegance to bend to casual style.

The artistic sensibility that influenced Penny's web design projects was disturbed. She looked around for an obvious location of the original staircase and, for a moment, she saw it—traditional, regular, functional more than decorative— like a gauzy overlay floating on top of the current one.

She blinked her eyes, and the image vanished. She repeated the old lady's words, "Don't be surprised at what you see and hear." Imagination, or haunting? Penny laughed but progressed carefully. She put her right foot on the first tread and steeled herself.

It creaked.

She held her breath.

Nothing. No weird sensation. No sense of foreboding.

She exhaled and went up the staircase to the second-floor landing. There, the railing continued along one side, overlooking the great room. There were four rooms on this level, and the doors were open, with sunlight filling each of them. In all this summer light, who could believe in things that go bump in the night?

Judging from the length of the hall, there was a master suite and three smaller rooms. Penny chose to save the master suite for last, like dessert after a meal.

In the smaller rooms, white plantation shutters were a contrast to the dark wood flooring that was used throughout the house. The two guest bedrooms, separated by a full bathroom, contained beds covered with handmade summer quilts, crisp sheets, stacks of fluffy pillows, and whitewashed bureaus. Despite the similarities, each room had a theme and color of its own. One room, painted a creamy gold, displayed a bowl of seashells. The other one, a child's room, was painted peach and decorated with teddy bears dressed in bathing suits.

As soon as she stepped into the master suite, Penny saw a major contrast. The room was massive and had French doors that opened to a balcony at the back of the house. Penny beelined to those doors, turned the glass knobs, and admired the trees and flowering bushes that enclosed the small backyard, making it seem more a retreat than a yard. She could envision herself sitting on the balcony in the morning with a cup of coffee while enjoying the beautiful view.

When she closed the doors, she noted the fancy brass key in the lock. She tried to remove it for closer examination, but it was stuck. However, as she tried to wiggle it free, the key moved as though on its own. But still, she refused to believe that it was anything suggesting a haunted home. The key problem was simply the result of age and humidity.

She looked around the bedroom. In this room, the preserved shiplap was painted sea green. White crown molding topped the walls, and similarly-cut wood had been used to frame the two large windows that bookended a mahogany four-poster bed with sheer curtains secured to each post. *House Beautiful* and *Coastal Living* meets *This Old House*.

She flopped down on the bed and imagined living in this house, with its balcony and proximity to the heart of the town.

She closed her eyes and might have napped except that she heard music. Not a recording. The simple song was being played on what sounded like an alto recorder. And it was coming from somewhere in the house.

She sat upright.

The song stopped mid-note.

The French doors flew open, sending a strong breeze into the room and startling her. *I locked those doors. At least, I think I did.*

The ties that had kept the bed curtains secured to the bed posts fell open, and the white sheer fabric panels lifted into the air and closed around the bed. Penny pushed aside one of the panels, walked hesitantly toward the French doors, and checked the balcony. No one was there. No one in the backyard below, either. She stepped back into the room. "I'm locking these doors," she shouted, not so much that she expected someone to hear her, but because by saying it aloud she assured herself that she had indeed secured them.

She stood back and waited. Would they fly open again? *If they do, I'm out of here.*

After a minute that felt like an hour, she reasoned that the lock was probably loose and that was why the doors had flown open. That would also explain why the key had turned so easily. No ghostly interference. Just something to be addressed if she bought this cottage.

Reassured, she wandered around the room, touching each item as though claiming it as her own. The smooth tops of the refurbished mahogany dressers. The soft texture of two velvet easy chairs on either side of a double-domed floor lamp.

She had sat for only a moment when she heard footsteps and noticed that the bed curtains were starting to move slightly, as though someone had walked past the room.

The hairs on her arms stood up.

Penny halted her imagination. Just as in the French door situation, there had to be a reason. *Of course!* The door to the hallway was open, and the real estate agent had probably arrived and come into the house. That could have allowed air from outside to waft up to the second floor.

She left the room and leaned over the railing. "Sherry?"

No one answered.

"I refuse to get creeped out. So, if anyone is nearby, identify yourself or go away," Penny said in the sternest voice she could muster. *I don't believe in ghosts, and I don't believe in haunted houses,* she reminded herself. Yet she returned downstairs for an easy exit, just in case she needed one.

While waiting for the real estate agent to return, Penny chose a chaise lounge that butted against the wall, making it easy for her to keep an eye on the entire ground floor. *I'm not afraid,* she told herself. *I just want to be safe rather than sorry. Someone other than Sherry might enter, and I don't want to be in a vulnerable position.*

She felt unsettled. She doubted that she would buy this place, regardless of its renovation and low price.

Sherry Allen arrived with a whirlwind entrance. "I am so sorry, Penny, for being later than I expected. Summer is a crazy time here at the beach. So …" She did a *Let's-Make-a-Deal* arm sweep. "What do you think?"

"It's interesting."

"Interesting?"

"What do you know about its history?"

The woman shrugged. "The current owners say that it was built in the late eighteenth century by a sailor who survived a shipwreck just off the coast in the Delaware Bay. A Dutch ship, *De Wolfshound.* That's all I know." She walked to the dining room table, opened her portfolio, and took out a contract. "So where should we start the bidding?"

"Somewhere else," Penny answered.

"Over coffee at the Coffee Tyme at the Beach?"

"I mean another house in Cape May, but not this place."

The agent acted shocked. "Surely you're kidding. This is such a deal. Move-in ready. And no need to repair or replace anything."

"It doesn't feel ... like home."

"Not like home?" Sherry plowed on. "I've got a great idea. Why don't you stay here tonight? There's food in the fridge and a coffee/tea station on the counter. Explore the town, watch a little TV, enjoy that master suite, and come to appreciate what a great value this is. Give it a try before you walk away from this opportunity to live in historic Cape May."

Penny was taken by surprise. When did a real estate agent ever allow a client, a total stranger, to have a sleep-over in a property for sale? And provide food and drink? She'd heard of agents taking clients to lunch to seal the deal, but stocking the kitchen? "Isn't it unusual to do that?"

"Not at all. Especially if a house doesn't sell right away, like this one should have, and would have if the owners had listened to me when setting the asking price. Now, they've put their total faith in me to do whatever I consider appropriate in helping potential buyers see the value of this home."

An obvious lie. The real estate agent must be expecting a huge commission if she can dump this house.

Sherry looked over her eyeglasses. "You're not afraid to stay here, are you?"

"Of course not."

"Sure?"

Penny fell for the bait. She accepted the challenge. To back away now would be to admit her fears. And she wasn't about to admit that even to herself. "Okay. But it doesn't guarantee that I'll change my mind about buying this place."

She noticed that the agent's face relaxed but something

about her eyes made Penny uneasy. Were the warnings given by the old lady next door valid? It didn't matter. Penny had accepted the dare. What was the worst that could happen? That her own skepticism concerning the existence of ghostly spirits would be forever changed?

After the agent left, Penny took a bit of her advice. She explored the downtown stores and enjoyed a walk on the beach. Although she wasn't planning to buy The Wolfhound, she decided that she definitely wanted to live within walking distance to the center of Cape May.

When she returned to the cottage, she stood at the bottom of the porch steps for a few minutes, considering whether she should go through with the dare to spend the whole night in the house. She felt awkward staying there without the owners' personal invitation. But she had something to prove to Sherry Allen—and to herself.

After an evening reading a few chapters of a comic romance and playing solitaire on her iPad, she took a deep breath and sighed. *Challenge accepted.* She checked the locks on all the doors and windows and left lights on everywhere in the downstairs living area, as well as the reading lights by the matching bookcases in the master suite. And, because of her earlier experience with the French doors, she moved the easy chairs against them. *Just in case.*

Though a bit uncomfortable, she decided to lie down fully clothed on the four-poster bed in the master suite. *No one will ever know that I slept here if I don't climb under the sheets.* She considered staying awake all night, but the full day of activities made sleep come easily.

She was standing on a boat, looking out over a smooth ocean. The breeze rustled her hair. Peaceful. She heard melodious music like a soundtrack that sets the mood in a movie. Yet, no one was nearby. She searched the boat everywhere. Not a soul onboard, despite the music. No other passengers. No sailors. She was all alone. Then, the wind whipped up, shredding the massive sails, and the white clouds in the sky turned dark.

She awoke with a start and saw that the easy chairs she'd put against the French doors were back in their places by the bookcase. The doors themselves were open and the night air was filled with the scent of rosemary soap and rum.

She rushed to the bedroom door but stopped abruptly when she saw a man standing outside the child's room. Why hadn't she heard him walk up the wooden stairs?

The man turned and looked directly at her. He was dressed in faded brown knee-breeches and a loose-flowing white shirt. His midnight-black hair hung loosely from the leather tie that tried to hold it in a ponytail. Okay, he was in historic costume. But what was he doing here?

"Who are you, and what do you ..." She stopped in mid-sentence when she realized she could see right through him.

He disappeared, then materialized directly in front of her.

"Don't hurt me," she begged.

The French doors slammed shut. The furnishings in the room disappeared and were replaced by furniture befitting the eighteenth century. Lamps became candles. Walls, unpainted natural shiplap.

She felt the pressure of his hands around her waist, though her mind insisted that none of it was real. It was a figment of her imagination. But her lips felt salty. And warm. As though she'd been kissed. The top of her hand was being caressed. He was leading her toward the bed. In romance books, this would be exciting and sexy, but she knew now that those stories were false. No woman would invite the sexual advances of a ghostly apparition, not knowing whether that being was a demon or simply a lost soul.

She wanted to run but was unable to move.

From inside her back pocket, her cell phone blared *Happy*, by Pharrell Williams. Her mother's ringtone.

Wind blew through the room. The French doors opened wide. Penny watched as the room reverted to its current time period, and sensation returned to her limbs.

She rushed from the room and toward the staircase. No sign of any being—ghostly or real. *It's over,* she thought.

"Hi, Mom. … Out of breath? I had to find my cell phone. … Yes, Cape May is beautiful as always. … Tired, yes. … Call you if and when I find my dream home here. … Love you, too." Then, after she hung up, what she hadn't said in the conversation. *Thanks, Mom. You may have saved my eternal soul.*

Penny awoke to the sun streaming through the side windows of the living area, surprised that she had fallen asleep at some point during the night. Granted, she was waking on the chaise lounge and not on the comfy bed upstairs.

She stretched and yawned. "I need coffee," she mumbled, and headed into the kitchen area to get some. She contemplated last night's experiences while she leaned against the counter listening to the sound of the coffeemaker. *Was it a dream? Did I walk in my sleep and end up downstairs, or had I actually been visited by spirits?*

When she returned to the living area, she was so startled that she almost dropped her cup.

She was not alone. An elderly woman—corporeal, not ghostly—was sitting on a chair by the farthest window. "I warned you," she said. Her tiny voice identified her as the woman from behind the porch screens of the neighboring house.

"You mean, you tried to scare me away by making up ghost stories."

"Not ghost stories." She nodded her head. "You met Charles, didn't you?"

Penny chose a seat closer to her. "Who is he?"

"You mean, who *was* he? An ancestor of mine. The seafaring captain of *De Wolfshound*. The story passed down through generations of my family is that he was quite the ladies' man until an English beauty, Ruth Morgan, the daughter of a minister, captured his love and anchored him to this house in Cape May, where he lived a land-bound life with faith-bound morals until she died giving birth to their son, Edward. He was enraged that the God his father-in-law preached would take the only woman he ever truly loved. So, Charles handed the infant to the midwife and returned to the sea. Whenever in port, he led a life of debauchery. Hence, Ruth's parents never let the boy know that Captain Charles Blackthorn was his father, nor did the captain ever try to connect with Edward Morgan except to bequeath him this house and all his wealth."

"*De Wolfshound*? Why did you lie to me, saying the house was named 'The Wolfhound' to scare away the spirits of the dead?"

"It's not a lie. Charles didn't name the house; his son Edward did. They say that Edward's hair turned completely white during his first night as the owner of the house."

A knock at the front door interrupted. "Penny, are you awake?" Sherry Allen called from outside the front door.

"Come in."

"The door's locked."

Then how did the elderly woman get in? Penny turned to check if the woman was still there. *At least she's real.* Penny unlocked the front door.

As was her style, Sherry Allen rushed through the door and directly to the dining table as though she had many tasks to accomplish in little time. "Ready to sign?"

Penny remained at the door. "Not really."

"Why?"

"I doubt you'll believe this."

"Try me."

"This house is haunted."

Sherry acted surprised. "Haunted? Who told you that?"

Penny gestured to the woman who was still seated by the window.

"Do I know you?" Sherry asked.

The woman didn't answer, so Penny provided the introduction. "She lives in the cottage next door."

The agent snorted. "Impossible. I don't know who this lady is, but she doesn't live next door. Charlene Morgan is dead. And with no children, no relatives as far as anyone knows, and no will, it's just a matter of time until that house is released from probate and goes on the market. I have a pair of clients who can't wait until that day so they can buy it, gut it, restore it, and make a big profit on its resale."

The elderly woman stood. "Gut it? Never." Her corporeal body became silvery, then transparent, and then she vanished.

After all that Penny had already been through, she was not frightened by this ghostly exit, but she was surprised that Sherry was unfazed, though still staring at the now-empty chair where the elderly woman had been sitting.

"Damned ghosts," the agent muttered, and ripped up the contract for the house. Then she zipped her portfolio and said, "There's a great house one block over. Why don't we go check that one out?"

Penny stopped her. "The key to this one is still up in the bedroom. Don't you want to get it?"

"Nope." She crossed to the front door. "I'll text the sellers, and they can find it themselves. Combat pay is not part of the deal. Now, let's go house shopping."

Nancy Powichroski Sherman's award-winning short stories have been published in *Delaware Beach Life, Fox Chase Review, Referential,* and in the following anthologies: *The Beach House, Rehoboth Reimagined, The Divine Feminine: An Anthology of Seaside Scribes, Beach Love,* and *She Writes: Visions* and *Voices of Seaside Scribes.* Her own collection of stories, *Sandy Shorts,* was awarded a regional first place by Delaware Press Association and a national first place by the National Federation of Press Women. Nancy looks forward to the release of follow-up collection, *More Sandy Shorts* (Cat & Mouse Press, 2019).

TAPESTRY

BY PHIL GIUNTA

Doctor Rayna Geary, planetary scientist, rested her elbow on the half wall overlooking the bustling boardwalk at Obie's By the Sea. It was her favorite spot for lunch. Here, she could let her gaze drift from the crowded beach and rolling surf to the distant horizon where the murmuring cerulean sea kissed a clear azure sky. "Wherever we go in the galaxy, it will never truly be home. Not like this. Not like Rehoboth."

Across the table, her husband of three years—and colleague for twice that long—leaned forward and cupped his hand over hers. "I know it's heartbreaking to leave, but it's even worse to suffer the effects of global food shortages, ocean dumping, and overpopulation. We both know it'll only get worse. Once we're settled aboard the ship, we can finally start the family we always wanted. We'll reach a new world in our lifetime. Imagine being among the first to live on an exotic beach overlooking an alien sea."

Rayna nodded. "That could be amazing." Intellectually, she knew Devin was right, but she didn't *feel* it. "I just … don't want to think about it until next week. For now, let's enjoy our town while we still can."

"Agreed. Walk on the beach after lunch?"

A blaring klaxon cut off Rayna's reply.

She opened her eyes and drew in a sharp breath. Clutching her stomach with a quivering hand, Rayna rolled over onto her side, wheezing from yet another anxiety attack. She slapped the touch screen on her bedside table to shut off the alarm. This had become an almost daily routine since she began dreaming about Devin two weeks ago, but this attack was the worst yet—and she knew why.

Once she had finally composed herself, Rayna pushed disheveled gray locks out of her eyes, tossed aside the covers, and slipped out of bed to face the day.

Captain Ethan Geary stood in his mother's quarters aboard the generation ship *Sagan* and watched the sun climb leisurely between gossamer clouds above a sparkling sea. The silhouette of a cargo ship drifted across the horizon while three seagulls circled above the empty beach below before landing at the edge of the surf.

Ethan heard his mother emerge from the kitchen behind him, but kept his gaze fixed on the digital tapestry. "Delaware coast?"

Rayna stood beside him. "Rehoboth Beach, to be exact. I programmed it in last month. Your father and I lived there for several years before you were born. That was our view almost every morning. I miss it ... almost as much as I miss him." She turned away. "Breakfast is served, space cadet."

Ethan stepped over to the dining nook to find a plate piled high with pancakes in the center of the table. He pulled out a chair and motioned for Rayna to sit. "Honestly, Mom, you didn't need to go through the trouble. We could have eaten in the officer's mess."

"I made pancakes for you a few days after we lost your father, remember?"

Ethan nodded solemnly as he took a seat across from her. "Thirty years ago, today. I didn't forget, Mom."

"It seemed appropriate that we share the same breakfast again."

Ethan raised his glass of orange juice. "To Dad ... and you."

Rayna lifted her coffee cup and tapped it against his glass. They observed a moment of silence, during which Ethan glanced at the sun hovering high above Rehoboth Beach before speaking again. "There's something else I meant to bring up before but never found the opportunity."

"Uh-oh. Sounds serious."

"It's about what Doctor Umoya asked you at your first nanotherapy appointment."

"Whether I want to be put into cryonic stasis when my ALS reaches the point of no return, in the hopes that a cure will someday be found."

"It's just something to think about. I don't need an answer immediately."

"Apparently you do. Otherwise, why bring it up today of all days?" Rayna finished her coffee and set the cup on the table. "Here we are sharing breakfast before this gorgeous sunrise aboard a starship whose purpose is to carry the human race to a new world, yet all you want to talk about is my eventual demise."

"Just the opposite, Mom. Our mission is to offer a second

chance at life for the human race—and that includes you. I can't think of anyone more deserving, and I'm not just saying that because you're the captain's mother. After all, you and Dad worked together to map this ship's course to a new Earth."

They ate quietly for another minute before Rayna finally replied. "I'll think it over. Of course, if I suddenly drop dead before then, all bets are off."

"You have a way with words, Mom."

"Comes with age, space cadet."

"Just one favor. Please don't call me that in front of the crew."

"I can't make any promises."

Lying on her side atop the examination table, Rayna flinched as the cold metal of the nanite injector pressed against the back of her neck and, a few seconds later, against the base of her spine.

"Sorry, doctor." Rutan Umoya, the ship's chief medical officer, pulled the injector away and straightened Rayna's blouse. "Nanotherapy is not the most comfortable procedure, but the good news is that your body is accepting the treatment. You can sit up now."

Rayna pushed herself up with relative ease. "I couldn't do *that* a month ago, but there's no way these microscopic robots floating around in my system can cure me?"

"Not yet, but we're working on it." Umoya leaned back against the counter and continued in a thick Kenyan accent. "So far, the disease is staying ahead of the treatment. As we discussed before, the nanites are programmed to stimulate the motor neurons from your brain to your spinal cord, and from there out to your muscles, thereby slowing their degeneration, but until such time as we can determine how to reverse the degeneration permanently, this is the best we can do. If we don't find a cure in time, I did confirm that you're eligible for cryostasis, if you so choose."

Rayna twisted her mouth into a wry grin. "Confirmed that with the captain, did you?"

Alone in her quarters, Rayna took a sip of synthetic wine and stared at the surging whitecaps lapping onto the sands of Rehoboth Beach, recalling her breakfast conversation with Ethan. *All you want to talk about is my eventual demise.*

She'd stopped weeping minutes before and wiped her face with a napkin. *Seems that's all anyone wants to talk about anymore.*

When her vision cleared, Rayna shot forward in her seat and narrowed her eyes at the tapestry. A trim young man no older than thirty-five stood at the edge of the water, staring at the boats on the horizon. His bronzed skin appeared even darker in contrast against his yellow T-shirt and khaki shorts. *Who the hell are you and what are you doing in my program?* As if in response to her thoughts, the man turned and made his way up the beach—straight toward Rayna. As he grew near, recognition dawned on her. It took another second for the shock to catch up with her brain.

In that time, he had closed the distance and now stood as if on the other side of a glass door. With a smile, he reached out to her, his hand passing *through* the wall and into the room.

Rayna screamed.

Ethan dashed into his mother's quarters before the doors had fully parted. The medical team was just finishing their examination.

"Report, medic!" Ethan barked.

Rayna waved her hand. "It's all right, *captain*. I'm fine. Just had a bad dream, that's all."

The senior of the two medics explained that the infirmary had received an alert from Rayna's health implant indicating a rapid pulse and sudden increases in blood pressure and adrenaline. "She seems to be fine now, sir, but we gave her a mild sedative to help her rest."

Ethan nodded. "Thank you."

With that, the medics departed, and Ethan took a seat beside his mother. "How are you feeling now?"

"I said I'm fine."

"So, tell me about this bad dream."

"There was no dream. I just told them that."

"Then what really happened?"

Rayna sighed and rubbed the bridge of her nose. "You won't believe it."

"Try me."

"Your father was here."

Ethan stared at her in silence for a moment. "Here? In your quarters?"

"In the tapestry."

"Which one? Rehoboth Beach?"

Rayna nodded.

"You *were* dreaming."

"I was wide awake, sitting here enjoying the sights and sounds of our old home town when he just appeared at the water's edge and trudged right up to the wall."

"And you didn't program an image of Dad into the tapestry?"

"Don't you think I'd remember if I did? I'm not *that* old."

Ethan held up his hands. "Just making sure. Then let's fire it up and take a look."

Rayna hesitated before pressing a button on the arm of her chair. On the wall before them, the sun peeked over the horizon, casting its saffron reflection on a softly undulating sea and illuminating a deserted stretch of beach.

"Wait for it," Rayna said.

Minutes passed. Dense clouds briefly obscured the sun. The dorsal fins of four dolphins broke the surface then submerged again.

"It should have happened by now."

"You told me that you've been dreaming about Dad on and off for the past few weeks," Ethan said. "Yesterday was the anniversary of his death. It's only natural that he's been on your mind more than usual lately."

But he reached out to me.

Ethan stood and made his way toward the door. "I have to get back to the bridge. I'll stop by to check on you later."

"No need." She turned off the tapestry. "Maybe you're right, space cadet. It was probably just a dream. Sorry for the scare."

Rayna found herself seated alone on the screened porch of the Royal Treat, astonished to see the place deserted on such a sweltering summer day. She glanced up just as Devin emerged from the entrance and placed two sundaes on the table before sliding into the chair across from her.

Rayna leaned forward. "I don't recall ever seeing business this slow here."

"I prefer it this way." Devin pointed his spoon at her sundae. "I can't believe you still like butterscotch over mint chocolate chip. Yuk."

"Don't knock it until you try it."

"Either way, I bet you can't get ice cream like this aboard the *Sagan*."

Rayna plunged her spoon into her sundae. "You got that right." She paused. "Wait. What did you say?"

"Why did you run away when I came to see you yesterday?"

"What are you talking about?"

"You screamed and turned off the tapestry. I might not be the most attractive guy, but you did marry me."

Rayna's spoon clattered to the table. "I thought you were a ghost."

Devin swallowed a mouthful of his Dusty Road sundae. "Why would you think that?"

"Because I watched you die when that plasma jet exploded

in orbit thirty years ago."

"It's been that long?" Devin looked away for a moment. "That explosion didn't kill me. It opened some kind of … portal to another dimension and I was pulled through. It wasn't long before I realized that I could manipulate my reality here through sheer thought. Don't ask me to explain it. It was chaos at first. I thought I was going insane. It felt like forever before I learned how to control it, but finally I did. Then I decided to recreate the town we once called home. This is Rehoboth Beach long before conditions on Earth deteriorated. It's nearly perfect in every detail, but it's missing one thing."

"What's that?"

"You." He took her hand in his. He felt warm, *alive*. Rayna squeezed his fingers. "Some time ago, I discovered how to reopen the portal at will. No explosion necessary. That's how I was able to reach out to you through the tapestry."

"So, you can come back?"

Devin shook his head. "I've lived here too long. If I reenter your reality, I'll be dead within hours."

"But I can come here?"

"Yes."

"Devin, I'm being treated for ALS. They've slowed its progress, but they can't reverse it. Ethan and Doctor Umoya are trying to convince me to enter cryostasis until a cure is found. If I come here, what will happen to me?"

"You'll be able to change your reality as I did; shape your own destiny. We could be together for eternity here."

"Will I be young again?"

"That all depends on you."

Around them, the Royal Treat began to dissolve. Wooden floors gave way to hard, packed sand, while the white ceiling faded to reveal blue sky. Husband and wife stood facing each other along the water's edge. Waves crashed onto the beach from where the street had been just seconds before.

"The *Sagan* is nearly out of range. I can only open the portal for short periods—maybe only one more time." As Devin stepped back, a wall materialized between them. He placed his open hand against it. Rayna did the same. "Devin? No! Please don't leave me again."

She awoke with a jolt, slumped on the easy chair facing the tapestry, but the only response to her plea was the shriek of passing seagulls above an empty beach.

Later that morning, Rayna sat on the edge of the examination table as Doctor Umoya prepared her injection. After a few minutes, she yawned and lay back.

Umoya glanced over his shoulder. "Are you feeling all right? I noticed your eyes were bloodshot when you came in."

"Doctor, has anyone reported any bizarre side effects to nanotherapy?"

"Such as?"

"Ever since I started these treatments, I've been having vivid dreams about my late husband. In one case, I actually saw him while I was wide awake."

Umoya shook his head. "To my knowledge, nothing like that has been reported."

"That's what I thought."

"But then everyone reacts differently while their bodies adjust to the treatment. Let me know if these experiences continue. For now, I can give you something to help you sleep."

Rayna responded with a desultory wave as she rolled onto her side. "No, I'll be all right."

This time, she didn't react as Umoya administered the injections. "Have you come to a decision on the cryostasis?"

"Been thinking about it. Depending on how long I'm in cold storage, there's a good possibility that if or when I'm revived someday, most of the people I know now will be long gone."

"That's always a risk."

At that, Rayna's choice became clear. "Today, I'm an old woman living in a metal crate hurling through space, spending my days staring at a digital image from a life I left behind, pining every day to be back there. That won't change ten, fifty, a hundred years from now when they pull me out of the freezer. The only difference is that I'll be a lonely old woman surrounded by strangers." She sat up and met Umoya's gaze. "I've made my decision, doctor."

"I understand you elected to stop the nanotherapy. May I ask why?"

Once again, Rayna's sitting room was bathed in the golden radiance of the morning sun. She sat before the tapestry, staring intently and ignoring Ethan's looming presence.

Finally, he moved in front of her, hands clasped behind him.

Rayna rose from her seat under his fuming scowl. "I knew you'd come charging down here sooner or later. Let's be honest, space cadet. What do I have to look forward to here? I'm dying, and frankly I'm tired of dealing with it. I have a unique opportunity to be with your father again in a place I wish I'd never left. When he came to see me last ni—"

"Stop it, Mom. Just stop." Ethan gently gripped her shoulders. "He did *not* come to see you or take you back to Rehoboth Beach. Those are dreams, nothing more. Speaking of which, didn't you and Dad share a dream of seeing the human race thrive on a new world? You talk about leaving, but don't you want to be there when we arrive?"

As he spoke, Rayna's gaze drifted over his shoulder.

"Mom, if you continue the nanotherapy and take advantage of cryostasis, you have a good chance of waking up on a new world that *you* helped discover."

Her lips curled into a smile as she sidestepped him and approached the tapestry.

"Mom, are you listening to—" After a double take, Ethan's eyes flashed wide. His exasperation drained away as he came face to face with a man who could have been his twin—a man Ethan had not seen since he was twelve years old. "Oh my God. Dad?"

Devin Geary, clad in a T-shirt and rumpled cargo shorts, raised his hand in a casual salute.

"He knows you're the captain now and he's very proud of you." Rayna placed a hand on her son's arm. "I have to go, space cadet. I don't have time to explain. Let's just say I'd much rather spend the rest of eternity with your father under the summer sun than alone in the deep freeze. Would you deny me this?"

"Of course not, but I don't understand. Where are you going? That's just a digital projection isn't it?"

"Someday, I hope you'll join us, but not too soon. Save the human race first. Rehoboth Beach will always be there."

With that, Rayna embraced her son, kissed him on the cheek, and stepped through the tapestry.

The bikini-clad woman walking beside her husband on the sands of Rehoboth Beach no longer feared any debilitating illness. With youthful hands unmarred by age spots, she scooped up a pair of seashells, marveled at her supple legs, and reached up to twirl soft, windblown locks of auburn.

In the distance to the north, two familiar concrete towers, monuments to an ancient war that never reached these shores, stood shrouded in the rippling haze of summer heat. Rayna took Devin's hand as she gazed from boardwalk, to beach, to rolling surf. She was home. "Are we really in the past?"

"Past, present, future." Devin shrugged. "Time has no meaning here. This place is eternal, as are we. It'll never change except as we wish it to."

"And we'll never have to leave again?"

"Never."

Ethan slid his hands along the tapestry but encountered only a solid wall. He backed away as he watched his parents—

younger than he'd ever known them—run hand in hand along the edge of the water until they disappeared from view. With a deep, shuddering breath, Captain Ethan Geary of the Earth ship *Sagan* drew himself to his full height and deactivated the tapestry. Before leaving his mother's quarters, he keyed in a series of commands on the control panel and smiled in anticipation of waking up the next morning to a Rehoboth Beach sunrise.

Phil Giunta's novels include the paranormal mysteries *Testing the Prisoner, By Your Side, and Like Mother, Like Daughters*. His short stories appear in such anthologies as *A Plague of Shadows, Beach Nights,* the *ReDeus* mythology series, and the *Middle of Eternity* speculative fiction series, which he created and edited for Firebringer Press. As a member of the Greater Lehigh Valley Writers Group, Phil also penned stories and essays for *Write Here, Write Now, The Write Connections,* and *Rewriting the Past*, three of the group's annual anthologies.

Phil is currently working on the second draft of a science fiction novel while plotting his triumphant escape from the pressures of corporate America where he has been imprisoned for twenty-five years. Visit Phil's website: www.philgiunta.com.

REHOBOTH BEACH IN CRISIS

BY CARL FREY

P lease hold the door," said a frazzled young woman in a gray business suit, struggling with an armful of computer equipment and cables. An older man with a long ponytail who was wearing flip-flops, shorts, and a sweat-stained Dogfish Head T-shirt stepped aside and held the door open, allowing her to pass. He looked her up and down approvingly. On the door someone had taped a sign, the same one that had been posted all over the community.

NOTICE

REHOBOTH NEEDS YOUR HELP!

COME SHARE YOUR IDEAS FOR SOLVING OUR TOWN'S CRISIS

JOIN YOUR FELLOW CONCERNED CITIZENS

MEETING TONIGHT – 7:00 P.M.

SECOND FLOOR CONFERENCE ROOM

REHOBOTH POLICE DEPARTMENT

REHOBOTH AVENUE

OPEN TO ALL

"Thank you." The woman nodded to her door opener, moving fast to avoid his stare. "It's just been nuts these past few weeks."

"You got that right, young lady. It's like the end of the world. I'm here, like a lot of the town's business owners, hoping we get this fixed before the summer season takes off. I've already had one setback so far this year and I don't need another."

Once she passed through the door, she turned her head over her shoulder and said, "I'm sure most everyone in town is concerned."

She backed away when the man in the T-shirt moved closer to her.

"I don't need more problems," he said, pointing at her as he spoke. "Earlier this season I lost a shipment of red food coloring. The drum I ordered fell off a barge coming down the Delaware Bay and I can't get a replacement for months, so I can only sell blue cotton candy to the summer tourists. Kids usually want blue, but their moms insist on red. They don't like their kids walking around with blue tongues. But now blue is all I got. I can see my cotton candy sales tanking this summer."

People continued streaming through the door, walking between them, making it difficult to converse. The woman gave the man in the Dogfish Head T-shirt a long last look and nodded her head slowly but said nothing more as she headed inside. She walked ahead, leaving him talking to himself.

A uniformed police officer motioned people toward an upstairs conference room where the mayor and other town officials had gathered around a dais. The wall clock read 7:05 when an intern in a crisp white shirt stepped up, faced the noisy crowded room, and picked up a microphone.

"Okay, we'd like to get started."

People settled into their seats and quieted down.

"I'm Frances Crick, aide to Mayor Jane Watson. I'll be facilitating this meeting. Thanks to all of you for coming on short notice. We are using this meeting to educate the community and ask for your support in resolving our crisis. We'll start with the educational segment of our meeting by asking Jamie Clerk Maxwell, doctor of zoology at the University of Delaware College of Earth, Ocean, and Environment in Lewes, to provide some background. Dr. Maxwell?"

The young woman in the gray business suit stood up from behind a laptop and LCD projector she had set up on the dais and smoothed her long, blonde hair. She faced a crowd that filled the room to capacity. A *Cape Gazette* reporter with a camera sat on the floor before the front row.

"Hello everyone and thank you, Frances. We'll start at the beginning."

She picked up the projector remote and clicked it to display a picture on the blank, white wall behind her.

"Let's talk about our problem. Here we have Exhibit A, *Limulus polyphemus*, a member of Chelicerata subphylum of arthropods ..."

Mayor Watson cleared her throat, leaned over, and whispered, "Doctor, can you give it to us in layman's terms?"

"Certainly, Madam Mayor. As I was saying, *Limulus polyphemus,* otherwise known as the horseshoe crab, is the subject under discussion. It is native to the Rehoboth Beach area, where it finds suitable breeding conditions. Anyone who has walked the beach here can find them at the water's edge, especially in the spring. Their shells often reach twelve inches in length, with a telson—I mean tail—that can be just as long. Ordinarily, they are harmless. Their unusual blue blood has useful medical applications that my group has studied for years."

Dr. Maxwell brought up a new picture.

"However, what we have in Rehoboth Beach now, as I am sure you are all aware and can see here, are hundreds of horseshoe crabs the size of Volkswagen Beetles. They are not only on the beach, but also have come inland. Once on land, they seem to have lost any desire to move and have parked themselves all over town. Many thought the crabs would die once they came on land—which might have created an even bigger problem—but volunteers from MERR, the Marine Education, Research & Rehabilitation Institute in Lewes, as well as the Rehoboth Beach Fire Department, have managed to keep the crabs alive with daily water sprays. If the crabs move at all, they do it in the cool of the evening. I have some more photos."

The projector displayed pictures of the giant horseshoe crabs. One showed children attempting to crawl on their shells and another showed a crab clogging the Penny Lane Mall. In another photo, a crab occupied a parking spot in front of Clear Space Theatre, the marquee announcing *The Rocky Horror Show*. Actors surrounded the parked giant crab, posing for a photo-op. The last picture showed a crab with its shell spray-painted "Follow me to Crabby Dick's" in large red lettering.

"I have spoken to the Crabby Dick's people and they insist

that, while they had nothing to do with it, they appreciate the free advertising. I also want to put to rest rumors that the giant crabs have abducted small dogs and children. There is no credible evidence to those assertions. That said, I ask everyone to keep their pets and children close and avoid annoying the crabs. As far as we can tell they are harmless, even if quite a bit larger than usual …"

An audience member turned to the woman next to her and said, "I hear that if you bring a picture of yourself posed next to the painted crab you can get a 10% discount at Crabby Dick's."

A man in a pinstriped shirt and poorly knotted tie stood up from his seat on the dais and started waving some papers.

"Mayor Watson, if I may …"

Frances Crick rose. "People, allow me to introduce Commissioner Curie, supervisor of the town's parking facilities."

"Thank you, Frances. This will just take a moment. I wanted to address the good doctor's comment that these menacing crabs are harmless. They are not harmless. While the crabs occupy parking spaces, the town is losing valuable parking revenue. I estimate that the city has already sustained a parking revenue shortfall on the order of, let me see, I have the numbers right here …"

The commissioner lost his grip on the papers and they scattered before the dais. Laughter erupted from the audience. Several audience members came forward to collect the fallen papers and in the process jostled the dais, requiring Dr. Maxwell to steady her projector. More laughter rose from the audience.

The mayor grabbed the microphone, stood, and said, "Thank you, commissioner, we will inform the budget committee that we expect a shortfall. But now I understand Dr. Maxwell has some important information to share. Dr. Maxwell, back to you."

The commissioner remained standing, waving a handful of bent papers.

"But parking revenues are vital to our balanced budget ..."

The mayor glared at the commissioner, who slowly sat, his mouth forming a pout. The mayor nodded to Dr. Maxwell.

"Thank you. I agree that the crabs have led to some increased costs for our community, but let me share with you some important new findings. Early this season, as part of our ongoing research, we tested the blood of some of the normal-sized horseshoe crabs and discovered that several of them had purple, not blue, blood. At first, we were excited, as we thought we had come across a new subspecies of horseshoe crab, but when we analyzed the blood, we found traces of erythrosine, otherwise known as the approved food coloring Red No. 3."

People in the audience began to talk to one another and reached for their cell phones. The man in the Dogfish Head T-shirt covered his face with his hands. Frances tapped on her microphone.

"Can we allow our speaker to finish? Dr. Maxwell, please continue."

"Those of you who live here year-round may recall that this spring we had what some called a red tide. For a brief period, the waters in Delaware Bay had a distinctly red cast. At the time we at the University of Delaware did not associate the red tint with a red tide—an algal bloom phenomenon—as the waters of the bay were much too cool and the color faded quickly. We did not test the waters of the bay for Red No. 3 at that time, and we do not know if there is a link between Red No. 3 and our giant horseshoe crabs, but our investigations continue. I can say that just tonight I received more information that supports the theory that our red tide was really a Red No. 3 spill.

"It is possible that exposure to Red No. 3 during the time the horseshoe crabs started to spawn triggered an unusual growth spurt that led to the current situation. Since the Red No. 3 has dispersed, I'm pretty confident that no more giant horseshoe crabs are likely to invade Rehoboth Beach. We continue to watch the waters. It could be that the crabs found the dye irritating and were reluctant to return to the water, so they took to the streets of Rehoboth."

Out of the corner of her eye, Dr. Maxwell noticed the man with the Dogfish Head T-shirt easing his way out the rear door of the meeting room. She smiled and, after a pause, turned her attention back to the audience.

"Our trolling underwater cameras see no more giant crabs offshore. As far as where we go from here, well, that's the reason for this meeting."

Frances stood up and said, "Thank you, doctor, for your analysis of the situation and for your lead-in to potential next steps. As far where we go from here, we are lucky to have with us this evening Colonel Mack 'Big Mac' Planck from the Air Mobility Command based at Dover Air Force Base. Colonel Planck?"

Big Mac, six feet six, sporting a buzz cut and wearing a neatly pressed uniform, rose from the audience and walked to the dais. He threw his shoulders back and held a microphone in a tight fist.

"Good evening, everyone. Earlier today Mayor Watson and I toured your wonderful town. I think I understand the situation and can propose a way that the US Air Force can attack your problem. I have already shared with Mayor Watson and the governor my proposed operational plan. We aim to deploy heavy-lift Chinook helicopters to transport the giant crabs to the Air Force Base in Dover, load them into one of our C-5 Galaxy aircraft, and then drop them far offshore, where the gulf stream will disperse them into the North Atlantic. We estimate that seventy-five percent of the two hundred or so giant crabs will survive this process. I consider twenty-five percent losses acceptable due to the unusual nature of this undertaking. It's just an estimate, as we have never done anything like this before. We just need the mayor to give us a go and our copter crews will move into action to execute what we are calling Operation Crab Net."

The mayor shook the colonel's hand and said, "We thank our military experts for their offer of help. I'm sure you can appreciate, colonel, that Rehoboth Beach will seriously evaluate your solution, but this meeting is intended to hear all possible solutions, so next I want to bring up Linda Pauling of CAMP Rehoboth."

A woman in the front row, wearing a summer dress and her hair in a thick braid, came up to the microphone, cleared her throat, and turned to the audience.

"Hello, everyone. While I respect the efforts of our military as much as the next person and don't want to minimize the problem that faces us, I would like to think that Rehoboth could find another solution that is more in line with the diversity and inclusion efforts CAMP Rehoboth champions every day, efforts that have made Rehoboth a more positive place to live. Let's all just take a moment to consider that in some ways these unusual creatures actually are enhancing Rehoboth. They have hurt no one. They have attracted scientists and media that have put our town in a favorable light. Please think about how we can accommodate these peaceful creatures who have existed and endured for hundreds of millions of years."

As the CAMP Rehoboth representative sat down, the audience started talking and raising their hands, asking to speak. Mayor Watson, her forehead beaded with perspiration, covered the microphone with her hand and leaned over to Frances.

"Frances, it's stifling in here and what's that noise outside? Can we close the windows and get the AC going?"

The mayor stood up, "Excuse me, folks. We're going to take a bit of a break here while we crank up the ventilation and try to cool off the room."

Frances covered her mouth slightly with her hand and tapped the mayor on the arm, "Sorry, mayor. The AC techs had to take the system down this evening for routine maintenance in accordance with the schedule in our contract. We didn't think of the AC maintenance schedule in the rush to arrange this meeting. The AC will be down for at least another hour. I'll see if we can turn up the fans. As far as the noise outside, the Heat just started up at the bandstand at the end of Rehoboth Avenue."

"Frances, why are we heating the bandstand in the summer?"

"Madam Mayor, we're not heating anything. Playing tonight at the bandstand, as part of our summer music program, is the doo-wop band, Lonnie Prickley and the Heat."

"Prickley? You don't mean—"

"I do mean. Lonnie Prickley is former mayor Arthur Prickley's cousin. As last year's mayor, he approved the music schedule for this year. Since he had already lost the election, former mayor Prickley took the opportunity to award a gig to his cousin."

Mayor Watson frowned. "I hate doo-wop."

"Sorry to hear that, but it's too late now to cancel their performance, and I'm told the Heat are pretty good. There's already quite an audience assembled. Apparently, the townspeople like the band. Ultimately, this could work in your favor, Madam Mayor."

"It could? Is everyone but me a doo-wop fan?"

At the rear of the meeting room, a crowd collected at the windows, pointing down on Rehoboth Avenue, shouting and taking photos with their cell phones. Someone opened a window and doo-wop filtered into the room. The mayor and the other speakers left the dais and went to a window to see what had everyone excited.

While the Heat played and a throng of people danced near the bandstand, the crabs started creeping toward the ocean, upsetting trashcans and folding chairs in the process. Dancers made way for a march of giant crabs and the band continued to play, oblivious to the crab exodus.

The mayor tapped Frances on the shoulder.

"Perhaps we should tell the band to stop before someone gets hurt."

Dr. Maxwell stepped between them and said, "Madam Mayor, I suggest we let the band play on. It's the first time we have seen the crabs move as a group. It's just a hunch, but I have a feeling that crabs do not have much affection for doo-wop. This offense to their musical taste appears to be driving them back to the sea."

Mayor Watson smiled widely and nodded.

"I knew there must be others who didn't like doo-wop. Okay, if it takes doo-wop to send the crabs back to where they belong, then I guess it's time to turn up the Heat. Frances, I approve an emergency appropriation out of the discretionary fund—whatever it costs—to pay Prickley for an additional set. I want these monster crabs out of here!"

"I'll get on it immediately, Madam Mayor."

As the band played on, the crabs slowly made their way to the shore and disappeared under the waters of the Atlantic.

Where the giants went afterward remains unknown, at least for now. Will they return to Rehoboth or will they come ashore somewhere else? Is the world safe from monster horseshoe crabs? Will they appear next spring to spawn more giant crabs? We wait and see. In the meantime, watch the waters. Watch the waters …

After Carl Frey retired from forty-one years working in flavor and fragrance chemistry, he hung up his lab coat, moved to Lewes, Delaware, and enrolled in writing courses at the Osher Lifelong Learning Institute. That leap led him to the Rehoboth Beach Writers' Guild and publishing a picaresque adventure/comedy novel—*Caldonia Cafe*. He currently leads Guild-sponsored free write sessions on alternate Monday mornings at the Rehoboth Beach Public Library and volunteers at the Cape Henlopen Bike Barn and the historic Overfalls Lightship. When not scribbling, Carl prepares ravioli from scratch and constructs wooden boats—rowboats, canoes and kayaks—that he self-propels along the Broadkill River and the Rehoboth-Lewes Canal. "Rehoboth Beach in Crisis" is his first contribution to a Cat & Mouse Press anthology.

I FELL FOR AN ICE-SKATING ALIEN

BY DAVID STRAUSS

A s I sit here writing these words beneath a night sky devoid of stars, a salty ocean breeze caressing my cheek, it comes to me that the events I am about to provide henceforth—and my participation in these adventures—happened quite by accident. All I'd wanted to do was spend a summer delivering pizzas and surfing in Ocean City, Maryland.

It began on an early Saturday morning when I found myself outside town, somewhere along Route 54 in the vicinity of Selbyville, browsing yard sales for old bric-a-brac. There hadn't been much to get excited about until I saw the strange-looking little creature staring back at me: a wooden tiki. I scooped it up and paid the kind woman two dollars.

As I began to pull back onto the road, I was almost struck head-on by a woman driving a bright-red Ferrari. Our eyes met for half a second before I steered my Jeep slowly around her car, the woman staring me down the entire time.

I shouldn't have let her in when I saw her again, standing in the doorway of my apartment. But she was a vision if there ever was one, this platinum blonde with smoldering eyes that stared right through me.

She glided—floated, I thought—right past me and across

the room to the bookshelf where I'd placed my newly purchased tchotchke.

"Who are you?" I asked.

"Caju Futura," she said without bothering to turn around.
"Medium."

"Medium," I managed to mumble, "you're anything *but*
a medium." And then, "would you mind explaining what
you're doing here?"

She turned to meet my gaze, and for a second, I thought I
saw the corners of her lips curl into a smile, as she explained
just what a medium was, but I'd be lying if I told you I heard
a word she said. All I could think of were those pouty lips
and how I longed to kiss them, to stroke that mane of hers,
to stare into the endless sea of her deep-blue eyes.

"Caju Futura," she said. "My name is Caju Futura." She
smiled seductively. "But you can call me Kitty."

I watched this dame, mesmerized.

Caju—Kitty—leaned in close to examine the tiki, her big
baby blues meeting its menacing eyes. She raised her hands
and moved them around the object, her long fingers flowing like the tentacles of a jellyfish, never once touching the
odd-looking little statue. Her body swayed slightly, as if in
a trance, and then she fell to her knees, blonde waterfall of
hair cascading to the floor, her torso like melted candle wax.

I stood above her, watching, terrified and transfixed, yet
somehow slightly aroused.

Kitty did not move for almost a full minute, then rose slowly to her knees, her sapphire eyes face-to-face with the evil
eyes of the tiki. She wrapped her slender fingers around the

object's small body and began to chant in a language I'd never heard before.

She stopped and stood in one graceful motion, a finger pressed to her lips.

"Someone's coming," she whispered.

I didn't hear a thing and was just about to tell her so, except when I turned to speak, she was nowhere to be seen. Kitty had disappeared.

In that moment, the door burst open and two tall men dressed in black suits entered the room. "Kukulkan," one said. "Where is it?"

His words were clear, but something in his tone was off, like a computerized voice. Although I couldn't move, chills ran up and down my spine.

The other man stood, long arms hanging at his side, and I could feel his eyes looking right through me, even though he was wearing dark sunglasses. I don't recall seeing his mouth open, but his words boomed with a force like thunder. "And I looked, and behold, the four wheels were beside the cherubim. … And their appearance was as one, the four of them, as if the wheel were in the midst of the wheel."

My head began to swim, and I began to feel dizzy. Next thing I knew, the lights were out.

When I woke, the men in black were gone, as was the statue.

But I did find Kitty, sitting alone at my kitchen table, helping herself to a cup of hot tea.

"What are you doing here? Where did you go? And who

were those guys?" I asked, trying to shake the woozy out of my head.

Kitty pushed a chair out with one of her long legs. "Better have a seat," she said. "Where did you find that statue?"

I eased myself into the chair and rubbed my temples. "Well, actually—I got it at a yard sale out on Route 54—but you already know that, don't you?"

She didn't respond to my question, but instead began to tell me a story. "During the first lunar landing, the astronauts were approached by a group of creatures from the dark side of the moon. That was the beginning of a long and complicated relationship."

"What?"

"NASA has been sending missions to the moon ever since. I mean, did you really think they just stopped going?"

Kitty answered her own question. "No. They've been going on a regular basis since that first landing. The thing is, NASA couldn't do it from their usual launch site in Florida."

"Then where? How?"

"Ever heard of Wallops Island?"

"Wait. Stop." My head felt woozy again. "What does that have to do with those guys—and what is a Koo-Koo Con?"

Kitty giggled. "Maybe I need to back up a bit. But first, maybe you should make yourself a pot of coffee because I've got quite a story to tell you."

"It began many years ago, long before the Europeans ever set foot in the Americas. Contact occurred simultaneously among many of the native communities of North and South

America—the Mayan, Polynesian, and Navajo, just to name a few. The stories from each of these cultures are basically the same: legends tell of a white-skinned man, who was known as a serpent god, a visitor from—"

"Let me guess, a visitor from outer space, right?"

"No, but nice try. Kukulkan emerged from the ocean and disappeared beneath the waves afterward. He was said to have blond hair and blue eyes, and he taught the Mayans about agriculture, medicine, mathematics, and astronomy."

"So—if no UFO, then what?"

She smiled, almost wickedly. Seductively. "Ever heard of a USO?"

"Huh?"

"USO—Unidentified Submersible Object."

"You mean the same as a UFO, only underwater?"

"You got it. Mankind knows less about the oceans of its own planet than it does the solar system. Think about that. Now, if there are no further interruptions, may I continue?"

I nodded, entranced.

"So, this man, this serpent god, traveled among the many tribes occupying this—and other—planets to bring peace and knowledge. But he also gave a warning to use resources wisely. He told a tale of a race of beings on the extreme edge of our solar system who squandered their natural resources and were forced to flee in search of an energy source just to keep their people alive."

And it was here I thought I noticed a sadness pass across Kitty's face.

"But it was to no avail. For although the Mayans—and others—used the knowledge of arithmetic and agriculture, of astronomy and architecture, they would ultimately fail to heed the warning given to each of them."

Again, sadness washed over her beautiful face.

"So, we watched and waited as differing cultures squandered resources and collapsed, watched as humankind fought for control of this planet. Revolutions, colonization, world wars. It wasn't until WWII had ended and the United States became the dominant world power that we attempted to try again. In 1954, contact was made with President Eisenhower to discuss a pathway forward for Earth. The United States was given access to some technology along with the understanding that it be used to keep peace in the world. In addition, a warning was given about the responsible use of resources."

Kitty paused to sip her tea. I'd already downed two cups of coffee and was dumping sugar into a third.

"Your government agreed to follow our guidelines, and for a while it seemed as if everything was going to be fine. It was our technology that allowed you to gain access to the moon, and it was on that first lunar landing that your astronauts made contact with another group of beings—a group far different from mine."

"So, like, you're an alien?"

Kitty ignored the question. "The other race had discovered a gem on the moon—Breccia-3. Although it looks something like what you people call an emerald, it is a powerful energy source. This other race told the astronauts that the Breccia-3 belonged to them, and that any attempt to take it would be considered an act of aggression. So, the astronauts left it, but now that your people knew what to look for, they launched a series of explorations and eventually discovered a piece of Breccia-3 on Earth."

My brain was humming with caffeine, adrenaline, and infatuation, but I had a sudden realization. Without saying a word, and with Kitty in mid-sentence, I left the table and wandered back to my bedroom. On the floor, beneath a pair of still-wet surf trunks, I found what I'd remembered. I returned with the green stone in my hand.

Kitty looked as though she might faint. "Where—"

"It fell out of the tiki when I brought it home. I was gonna superglue it back in, but those guys came and took it before I got a chance." And then, like the cylinders of a lock clicking in to place, it all made sense. "Wait, *this*?"

Kitty nodded.

"This little green rock is a powerful energy source? And those guys, those men in black, they were really here for this?"

Again, she nodded her head slowly.

"And let me guess, these guys, these MIB, they're from that planet, that other planet that used up all its resources?"

"So you were paying attention."

"And?"

Kitty scooted her chair right next to mine, her golden locks brushing against my cheek. "And they'll do anything to retrieve it. I told you this other race was different from mine. They do not value the resources found on the planets of this solar system."

And without me even realizing, Kitty had taken the gem-stone from my hands and now held it between her slim fingers. "But if they were to take hold of this ..."

"What?"

A cloud of sorrow passed across her face. "Let's just say it would provide them the energy to do as they wanted. They'd be almost unstoppable."

"So, what do we do with it?"

Kitty rolled the unpolished rock in her hand. "We hide it."

"So, just one more question."

Kitty grinned. "Go ahead."

"You're not really a medium. You're an alien, aren't you?"

"No, I'm not a medium. I'm the featured ice skater at the Carousel Hotel. And yes, I am an alien."

"Cool," I smiled. "I think I'm in love with an ice-skating alien."

I grabbed the red pizza delivery bag and walked out through the back of the store to a bike rack along the edge of a canal, where I strapped the bag onto a beaten-up old beach cruiser, checked the address, and began to pedal up Coastal Highway.

Across the street from my place of employment, the Carousel rises twenty-two stories against the night sky, the name of the hotel spelled out in large letters that run down the center of the imposing tower, glowing brightly in blue. A smaller sign sits along the highway and the entrance to the parking lot, the marquee informing the public of a nightly ice show, featuring my very own Kitty Futura.

I rode past, staring at her name in lights, and wondering when I'd get to see her again, my head full of questions.

The city was alive and buzzing and the breeze was warm, almost friendly. I glided back into Pizza Tugos, feeling so good after catching a sweet tailwind and a string of green lights from 142nd to 120th that I'd almost forgotten about the little encounter two days ago with the men in black. Almost.

Another pie was waiting for me, and as I strapped it onto the carrier on the rear of my bike, I happened to look across the street at the Carousel, looming like a giant against a hazy sky lit by light pollution. As I began to take off, I noticed that the lights spelling out the name of the hotel had gone dark. They blinked on and went out again. When they came back on a few seconds later, only the *C, A,* and *U* were illuminated. And while the *C* and *A* glowed brightly, the *U* kept flickering so that every other second or so only about half of the letter could be seen, kind of like the letter *J*.

CAJU. That ice-skating alien had taken possession of my heart—and now my head. I'd been pedaling up and down Coastal Highway for over seven hours now, breathing exhaust fumes and subsisting on nothing but slices of cheese pizza and Dr. Pepper. I shook the cobwebs from my head and glanced back. *CAROUSEL.*

I put my helmet down and pedaled into a nasty headwind that I swore wasn't there just a few minutes ago, determined to figure out what the hell was going on. I could hear the faint crashing of waves, the unmistakable sound of a new swell arriving, maybe just in time for a little dawn patrol after work.

After cleaning up and counting tips, I emerged from the back of the store, walked my bike across an empty Coastal Highway, excited to see the pounding surf I'd been hearing all evening.

Looking up at heavy clouds racing across a disappearing night sky, I could see that the lights running down the front of the hotel had gone dark again. And when they came back on, I did not see *CAJU*. This time it spelled *CAR*. The word began to blink faster and faster, on and off: *CAR, CAR, CAR*.

I spun just in time to see an old black Cadillac barreling up the bus lane, directly at me. Knowing I couldn't outrun it, I ditched the bike and sprinted through the Carousel's parking lot, through the front doors and into the lobby looking for help.

Nothing. The place was quieter than the boardwalk in a February snowstorm. And so, for no reason, instinctively I headed for the ice rink in the atrium of the hotel. I didn't know what I thought I'd find, but the place was dark and empty and cold, just like the sinister grins of the men in black who now had me surrounded, their eyes glowing like moonlight off the surface of the ocean.

Before I could escape, they pinned me facedown on the ice, and used my forehead as a battering ram.

"Where is it?" one of them hissed.

"You'll have to be a bit more specific," I replied, as best I could with my head being slammed against the ice. "*It* is a pronoun and you've not referenced a noun here, so I'm not quite sure what *it* is, and therefore can't know where *it* would be."

Crack—I so loved my skull. Crack!

"The gem, where is it?"

"Better, much better. Now, how about an adjective? What color gem, for instance."

Crack!

It was on this third crack, when my head bounced off the rink, that I spied *it*—and *it* was encased in the ice far enough below the surface that it would have been safe if my head hadn't started to break through the ice.

As quickly as I could, I used my left hand to cover the spot, the *it* spot, while singing the lyrics to *Surfin' Bird* as loudly as I was able.

Singing might have been an odd reaction, but it was odd enough to cause the MIB to pause the skull cracking and to attract the attention of the night security guard.

And when the guard found me, I was still screeching the words as loudly as I could, a cauliflower growing out of my forehead. Unfortunately, the perpetrators had vanished into thin air.

But the gem, the gem was still solidly encased just where Kitty had hidden it.

"I'm sorry about your head," Kitty purred sympathetically.

My forehead throbbed with the pain of an endless hangover. "You should see the other guy."

"Yeah?"

"Yeah, well in this case the other guy is your ice rink, and I beat it up pretty good." I paused. "Speaking of, I saw our little green friend buried in the ice, and I think we need a plan before somebody gets hurt, namely me."

Kitty smiled. "Agreed. The sooner I can get it out of here, the better for everyone."

The plan wasn't much, but it was the best we could do on short notice.

Kitty balanced herself on the handlebars of my trusty old beach cruiser like some life-sized hood ornament, her blonde hair flapping against my face as I tried my best to pedal south down Coastal Highway. We glided to a stop just outside of Seacrets, a popular bar in town. I grabbed Kitty's hand and led her to the rear of the long queue of tourists waiting to gain entrance. I'd be lying if I said that I wasn't feeling a bit satisfied by our hands being locked together.

The black Cadillac cruised into the parking lot, its engine growling like a jungle cat waiting to strike. The passenger door opened, and a tall man dressed in black stepped slowly from the vehicle.

Kitty squeezed my hand and as the car pulled away to find a parking spot, we sprang into action. I pulled her to the side where my friend Joshua, who also happened to be a bar back at Seacrets, was waiting. He led us through a side entrance, where we found ourselves immersed in a world of fantasy: reggae music and bars made from old boats sunken into the sand, thousands of sweaty bodies packed tightly together, every happy one with a Rum Runner or a Dirty Banana in their hands.

Joshua took us through the kitchen and out toward Assawoman Bay, where a long pier led out to the water. At the end, a boat was waiting, *Pizza Tugos* emblazoned in bright-red letters along the yellow hull.

"Hop in," Scott said.

Soon, we were out of the inlet and into the open waters of the Atlantic Ocean, the men in black nowhere in sight.

"I hope you know what you're doing," Scott grinned, his gaze fixed intently on Kitty's pretty face.

He cruised the vessel just offshore, managing the small swells with ease, the lights of Ocean City fading with each nautical mile. My boss glanced at a piece of navigational equipment and stared toward the beach, where all you could see were small black dunes silhouetted against a dark sky.

"You sure this is the place?" he said to Kitty. "Wallops Flight Facility?"

"Perfect." Only it came out *purrrrrfect*, and her eyes were glowing like they'd been lit by a blue flame.

Just then, the surface of the water began to bubble, a greenish-white light rising from the depths. I looked at my alien, glowing and radiant, her huge smile growing devilish.

"USO, I presume?"

As the craft rose from the ocean and Kitty began to step from the boat onto a platform of swirling light, two figures emerged from the cabin of Scott's boat. Two men in black.

Kitty's smile turned into a sneer and she growled at the men as she tried to leap from the vessel. I stood to block their way, but Scott tackled me, and the men stepped over us—floated over us—and onto the platform, where they took hold of Kitty, the gem spilling from her hand onto the deck of the boat.

Only it wasn't Kitty. The men in black were holding, what can best be described as a six-foot praying mantis with blue eyes and blonde antenna, sticking out from the top of its head. She—it—was wriggling uncontrollably and hissing so loudly I thought my eardrums were going to explode. A stream of black bile spewed from its mouth, covering all of us in a blanket of liquid stench. My eyes locked with hers for just a second and then my head began to spin like one of those lumps of dough Scott tossed when making pizzas.

The last thing I remember about that night was the sound of Scott's voice, his hearty laughter. "Man, I hate dating aliens. Nothing but trouble. There was this seven-foot Venusian—"

"You mean she played me like a cheap Atlantic City slot machine?" I shook my head back and forth. "And the whole time she was just pulling my lever."

The men in black smiled. "We'd been closing in on the missing gem for a while now. We knew it was in the vicinity, but for some reason it kept eluding us. In fact, we just missed you at the yard sale. When we recovered the tiki from your apartment and found the gem was missing, we knew we needed to keep an eye on you. More importantly, an eye on her. Our team intercepted a transmission to her people asking to be rescued, so we knew they'd be sending a craft to extract her."

One of the men chuckled. "We figured one of you had the stone, but we couldn't locate where it was. We had teams of men in black all over Ocean City—your boss being one of them. That ice rink turned out to be the perfect hiding spot."

I had a million questions. "But how did the most powerful energy source in the solar system end up in a tiki?"

"Who knows. We do know it went missing sometime toward the end of the Cold War. How it ended up here?" He shrugged.

The other man spoke. "Everyone from all reaches of the galaxy wants to get hold of it." He sighed. "We still don't understand its full potential."

I looked at my little tiki sitting quietly back on the book-shelf. "And Kitty?"

"We've dispatched a team to attempt to capture her ship, but we're pretty sure they're long gone. Kitty, aka Caju, aka Xtaabay, is wanted by the Galactic Counsel for crimes against civilizations. It was her people who were waiting for the astronauts on the dark side of the moon and it was her people who used all the resources from their home planet. When they heard of the discovery of this gem in the jungles of Guatemala, they immediately began to search and were determined to take it—to use it, one way or another."

His partner spoke softly. "Resource or weapon."

Scott gave me a week off, paid. He told me to go ride some waves, to sleep in, to check out some yard sales—and to get the alien out of my head.

Three out of four ain't bad.

David Strauss grew up visiting the beach, spending his summers in Clearwater Beach, Florida, and Ocean City, Maryland. He spent his college years living and working in Ocean City, where he delivered pizzas on his bicycle. David has had poetry and short stories published in *Damozel, Self X-Press,* and *Dirt Rag* magazines, and in *The Boardwalk, Beach Nights,* and *Beach Life.* He has also published two novels, *Dangerous Shorebreak* and *Structurally Deficient,* through CreateSpace. He teaches US History until he can retire to the beach.

THE DARK RIDE

BY LINDA CHAMBERS

When I was nineteen years old, I spent the summer working a pier in one of the beach towns in the lower section of the Jersey Shore, a real carny type of town. Never mind which one—nothing to look at now—Hurricane Sandy took out most of it. Sometimes I'd be in a booth; sometimes I'd work a ride. In the beginning, I divided my walks home evenly between the streets and the beach itself. Either option provided time to have quiet conversations with friends who were on their way home as well. The boardwalk? Way too wicked and crazed, even by the time I got off work. I was there to stockpile cash for college, not spend it on beer and weed.

The following year, I got a job in O.C. —Ocean City, Maryland—at the Candy Kitchen, Atlantic Ave. and the boardwalk. I was of age, so they put me on the night shift where I could close out.

Back then, the action was all at this end of town; the block upon block of high-rises you see now were just holes in the ground, foundations, a portent of things to come. The main amusement pier faced the Candy Kitchen, and what I hadn't considered was the crowd pouring off the pier at closing time. Young. Wild. Drunk. That was a challenge, so I handed in my pink uniform and little white apron and went back to the pier. Better to watch them stagger *away* than *toward* me. Since

I had experience from the summer before, I moved quickly from spinning the wheel to shooting the ducks, to tossing the ring, to grappling with giant stuffed animals. Problem was, I still liked the partying a little too much. I wound up with a lot of hazy memories and not much more.

The following year, I reevaluated. I'd partied my way through Jersey and Maryland, so now it was time to visit Delaware. I decided on Rehoboth Beach. Nice town. It's the kind of place you might visit and think about settling down in.

I thought about getting a job at Candy Kitchen, as I'd already done that, and my boss in O.C. had liked me. I considered Grotto Pizza and the waitress thing. I thought about bartending—a lot of money in that. I thought about applying to one of the fancier stores off the boardwalk. There was a bookstore, too, which looked nice.

But I liked *excitement*. You can take the girl out of the carnival, but you can't take the carny out of the girl.

I liked the whooshing sound of cars rocketing around a track, and the screams of terror and glee; I liked the game booths and the workers enticing the passersby to take a chance, spin the wheel, hit the target. I liked the smells of cotton candy, peanuts roasting, pizza, boardwalk fries heavy with vinegar, fudge, and popcorn. I liked the glow of neon as the sun set, growing gradually brighter and brighter, pulsating in the night sky as darkness fell.

Even back then I liked the dark.

I got a job at Funland.

Compared to the excesses I'd experienced the summers

previous, Funland was going to be a breeze.

There was an outdoor section off the boardwalk with bigger rides and an indoor section that was great when it rained. There were bumper cars and Skee-Ball, Whac-A-Mole and pinball machines, arcade games and booths.

This was also where you found the dark ride. It was— is— called the Haunted Mansion.

Night shift during the week usually had two workers. Sam—my shift partner—and I took turns handling the various jobs. We helped the folks get in their seats, which were suspended from the ceiling and moved on a sort of cable-car track. We strapped them in, gave them instructions, made sure everything was secure, and then cranked the lever that started them on their way. If a car stalled (which was rare; the ride was pretty new then), we were responsible for going inside the tunnel, pushing past the hanging skeletons, the swooping vampire bats, and the hands and heads that projected from the sides of the walls; stepping over the coffins that opened and tilted their contents up for display (remembering to hold our ears when we passed the loudspeakers); and getting things going again. There were some genuinely scary moments during the ride, and it was also our responsibility to go in and help any passengers that got so frightened they tried to get out of the car.

It was late July, a night like any other ... because that's always how they start.

This time, there was a child's cry from inside and then a man's voice shouting: "Stop the ride!" with real panic in his voice.

Sam and I looked at each other and did a quick "rock, paper, scissors," which I lost. He pulled the emergency lever down, and as he requested patience from those waiting in line, I switched on my flashlight and went inside, along the edge of the dark, winding tunnel.

There were three teens in the chair several yards behind the one I needed to get to. They'd already pissed me off when they'd clambered into the chair at the entrance, overly boisterous, shoving each other, and laughing too loud.

"It's all right, sir, don't worry, I'm coming!" As I passed the three boys I added, "Please, we'll be moving in a minute, just stay calm."

They snickered and snorted. I ignored them and continued, shining my light ahead.

Now I could see that the problem was a little girl. She'd been very excited as I'd seated her and her dad at the beginning and now, apparently, had had too much of a fright. It happens. Usually, though, the child is cringing and wailing in the seat. *This* child had managed to wriggle out of her seat belt and the seat itself, because she was out of the car, standing on the platform at the edge of the track. She was still, transfixed, staring off into the darkness.

Her dad, on the other hand, was wildly cursing at his own seat belt and the car was swinging as he struggled to get out.

"You just stay right there, sir," I said, "I'll handle this. Not to worry."

More sounds from the car behind. I could hear the car creaking. "Don't move, please!" I snapped back at them.

To the girl I said, soothingly, "C'mon, honey, there's a good girl."

She remained still.

I said, "The ghosts are scary, but they're not going to hurt you. Nothing to be afraid of —"

"It had a face," she interrupted, peering into the darkness.

"Oh, it's a stupid face, it's really silly if you look close enough at it."

"Not *that* one," the little girl said.

The boys in the chair behind were beginning to hoot and holler and make spooky sounds. They were urging me to "hurry up" and asking, "how long is this stupid ride, anyway?" The panicked father of the little girl was still trying to unbuckle his seat belt; he was now less concerned about his daughter and more focused on taking a fist to the boys behind him.

"Sir, please," I said to him. "It's all right. Just ignore them." I turned back to the girl and said, "If you get back in the seat with your dad, I'll tell you what I'll do. You come back later, and I'll take you behind the wall and show you how stupid the ghost is."

This intrigued her. I looked at her dad, eyebrow raised. It will be late, I mouthed. He nodded and looked relieved. He thanked me profusely, as I settled her back in her seat.

"Let's go!" I shouted, and the ride jerked to a start. As the second car passed me, I trotted along beside it, shone the light directly into the boys' eyes, and hissed, nastily, "That little girl was *scared*. If her dad doesn't beat the crap out of you when you get out, *I'll* find someone who *will*," which shocked them into silence as they were carried through the curtain.

As the cars disappeared around the curve, it struck me that the little girl hadn't seemed all that frightened.

Dad and daughter appeared as we were shutting down for the night. I could see her more clearly now—red hair and freckles and bright-blue eyes. She was wearing one of those matching short and shirt ensembles, very popular at that time. Blue top and red shorts, both splattered with tiny white stars and fishes. Dad had a medium-sized teddy bear tucked under one arm.

"I thought she'd forget," he said wearily. "Not Nancy. Go ahead, honey," he said to her. "You said you wanted to—"

"Can we go in now?" Nancy said to me, eyes shining with excitement.

"Sure," I said. I turned to Sam. "I'll finish inside. You close out."

"My wife is gonna kill me," the little girl's dad muttered, lighting a cigarette.

The generator lights were on in the tunnel. I held out my hand; Nancy looked at it disdainfully.

"Oh, yes, you *are*," I told her, and she sighed and took it reluctantly.

We trudged through the tunnel until Nancy stopped.

"Here," she said. "It was here."

"Okay," I replied. I handed her the flashlight. "Hold this. And stand back."

She obeyed. There was a trigger on the track that engaged the ghost dummy. I stamped my foot down on it with enough force to part the folds of the black curtain and propel the dummy forward. I flung my arms round it and pulled it into the light so she could see its white painted face, black holes for eyes, and plastic skeleton hands. As I dragged it forward, dust billowed up my nose and I sneezed; one of its fingers brushed painfully across my cheek.

"Here you go," I huffed. The thing was heavier than I expected it to be. "See? Nothing to be afraid of."

The beam of the flashlight wasn't on the dummy; it was bouncing off the curtains. It landed on the opening in back behind them. There were numerous openings throughout the ride; they led to a narrow walkway so workers could access the mechanisms that operated the displays.

"Nancy?"

"It wasn't *that* one," she said. She was peering beyond me, aiming the beam at the opening. She stepped forward.

"Whoa, hang on there!" I said. She halted. I eased the dummy back against the wall and turned to her. "This is the only one, honey," I said. "This is what you saw."

She shook her head, still staring at the opening. "No, it *wasn't.*"

"I swear, this is the only one—"

"*No,* it had a face."

"There's nothing else back there—"

"Nancy!" her father bellowed from outside. "Let's *go.*"

"On our way!" I shouted back. "Let's *go,*" I repeated.

She'd shifted her gaze from the opening to me. In the generator's half-light, her eyes were luminous. She tilted her head to one side and studied me briefly before slowly nodding her head. She was giving in, as children usually do, because they have to. She was bowing to the stronger of us, to me, the grown-up, and to her father's command from outside. Yet it was absolutely clear to me that *I* was the one who was wrong, and she'd made the adult decision to simply let it go. *She* knew the truth, not me. It was as though she'd made the whole argument in her head and, knowing she would never be able to convince me of it, she simply gave up trying.

"Okay," she said, holding the flashlight out to me.

As I took it, she said, "Your cheek's bleeding."

She turned and trotted toward the entrance. I turned, too, and looked back at the curtain. Most of it had fallen over the opening in the wall. I lifted my arm and stretched out my hand to pull it aside.

The hand flashed out from the darkness, its pale skin white against my deep summer tan; the fingers that curled around my wrist were slender and beautifully shaped but strong, so strong …

I gasped.

I heard Sam as though from a great distance. "You good in there?"

I felt my heart pound. It was in my chest and in my ears.

"Sam," I whispered.

The hand that encircled my wrist drew me through the curtain. He was taller than me; I had to look up. Now I understood what Nancy had seen, what had beckoned her forward. His eyes were gray. Those eyes locked me to him; I couldn't look away. He took hold of my chin and tilted my head to one side. He leaned forward and pressed his lips against my cheek, kissing it languidly, leisurely. His mouth drifted down my cheek to my throat. Something cold and sharp brushed my flesh.

Your cheek's bleeding ...

I heard Sam again, but he was miles away; the few yards that separated the outside of the ride from its dark center stretched all the way to the ocean, and what must have been an impatient shout was barely a whisper.

Something like, "You good?"

He lifted his head. His eyes were as luminous as Nancy's.

I thought of my life. I thought of home. I thought of school and the plans I'd made. I couldn't remember exactly what they were.

"Yes," I said and then, realizing Sam couldn't hear me, raised my voice. "I'm good."

"Okay. See you tomorrow. Don't forget the lights."

Silence.

We were still staring at each other. I thought I saw a question; maybe I did, maybe I didn't. In any case, I answered it.

"I want the dark ride," I whispered, and arched my neck.

He obliged.

That was well over forty years ago. At several points during our time together I would insist he tell me whether he had, in fact, given me a choice. He always said he had; had I said no, he assured me, he would have moved on. We parted on the eve of the millennium. I've caught glimpses of him since then, but we've traveled different roads. He was already many years older than me and had seen so much. I think he is waiting for me, though.

I returned to Rehoboth two years ago. I won't tell you exactly where, not that it matters. For forty years, I've considered it my hometown, the place I always thought of when far away. This is where I was born in the truest sense of the word. I always knew I'd go back, the way people do after so much time away.

It's early August, so I pass a lot of vacationers as I walk the boards. On a beautiful night like this there are crowds, but I don't mind crowds. I have a drink outside, at the Boardwalk Plaza Hotel. The ocean is noisy and the moon ripples across the waves. When I finish, I go down to the beach and walk all the way to Funland.

I stand at the edge of the boardwalk and peer across it, across the noise and the laughter, the shouts and giggles, into Funland itself.

I am drinking it in; it makes me happy.

Something shifts; something filters through; my senses are far beyond yours. What you might feel standing next to someone, I feel from yards and yards away. This starts as a tingle on my skin, something cold that wriggles across my arm. Then a sound comes through.

I cross the boardwalk. Now I'm inside Funland.

I swim through the crowd.

The Haunted Mansion has a long line in front of it, but I'm not here for the ride. Whatever is drawing me closer is level with the ride itself; I'm tracking it from where I stand.

One ride is ending. More shouts and laughter as a family

disembarks. The feeling is very strong now and I step closer.

There's a little girl with red hair struggling with her seat belt. She is impatient to get out. A middle-aged woman, already on the platform, is helping her with it. Once free, the child pushes off and the woman catches her, lifts her, hugs her close, and whirls her around. They are facing me now. The child is struggling; the woman is laughing.

"Oh, Gramma!" The little girl finally wriggles free and runs off the platform as the woman straightens up, her face still luminous with love.

Forty-odd years ago she was much like her grandchild; even now, I can see in her face happiness, good things, and adventure, her still-bright-blue eyes reflecting a life well lived. There is more gray than red in her hair, but it is thick and long, pulled back in a careless ponytail.

I, on the other hand, look exactly the same as I had the night I'd pulled her back from the curtain, nearly a half-century ago.

Someone close by says, "Nancy!" She doesn't move.

I don't need to hear her name; I recognize her. The shock is, *she* recognizes *me*.

She freezes, and so do I.

It's been many years since I've felt fear, but I feel it now. This life I've carefully constructed is built on a series of slender threads. It works because I am never in one place for long. No one knows me. I have several options, and I flip through them as I watch her emotions sweep across her face.

A man is beside her now, holding the little girl's hand. Nancy's husband. He touches her shoulder and she gasps. Then she smiles at him. They begin to move past me. She pauses and lets him walk ahead.

She says quietly, "You saved my life."

I wait until she is swallowed up by the crowd and then I move in the opposite direction, out of Funland, to the boardwalk, to the beach. The moonlight is shifting across the waves and I am pondering a new thought:

He always swore he gave me a choice. I believed him.

He said, "Had you said no, I would have moved on." But he was hungry; I know all about that hunger.

I believe *this* is the answer to the question I never asked:

"Had you said no, I would have taken the child …"

Linda Chambers teaches playwriting and screenwriting in the Literary Magnet Program at George Washington Carver Center for the Arts & Technology. Over the past year, her children's play *Little Red* was produced, two of her short screenplays, *To Be Or Not To Be* and *Welcome to Our School,* were filmed by the Young Filmmakers Workshop, and the first part of her fantasy novel, *The Swords of Ialmorgia,* became available on Amazon Kindle. She directs frequently in the Baltimore area and is writer/director of a one-woman show about Mary (Mother Jones) Harris. She looks forward each summer to spending as much time as possible on the Delaware beaches.

Want to Write Stories Like These?

Cat & Mouse Press Resources for Writers

How to Write Winning Short Stories

Write short stories with confidence after reading this practical guide that includes developing a theme and premise, choosing a title, creating characters, crafting realistic dialogue, bringing the setting to life, working with structure, and editing. Submission and marketing advice is also provided.

The book is perfect for anyone who is considering writing a short story. It will give beginning writers a practical playbook for getting started and help experienced writers build their skills.

Writing is a Shore Thing **Online Newspaper**

Writing is a Shore Thing is a free weekly roundup of the top writing advice and tips from experts. This paper is packed with useful information on dialogue, character development, setting, and theme, as well as editing, submitting, and getting published. It can be accessed online at www.writingisashorething.com. Subscribers receive an emailed summary when the paper is published each week. To view or subscribe, go to: www.writingisashorething.com.

If you enjoyed *Beach Pulp*

Sandy Shorts and *More Sandy Shorts*

What do you get when you combine bad dogs, bad men, and bad luck? Great beach reads. You'll smile with recognition as characters in the stories ride the Cape May-Lewes Ferry, barhop in Dewey, stroll through Bethany Beach, and run into the waves in Rehoboth.

The Sea Sprite Inn

Jillian has lived through more than her share of tough times, but leaps at a chance to reinvent herself when she inherits a dilapidated family beach house. Now, along with bath towels and restaurant recommendations, she offers advice, insights, and encouragement—with a side dish of humor— as owner of The Sea Sprite Inn in Rehoboth. As guests come and go, each with unique challenges and discoveries, Jillian learns to trust her instincts and finds a clear path to her future.

Rehoboth Beach Reads Series

These anthologies are jam-packed with just the kinds of stories you love to read at the beach. Each contains 20-25 delightful tales in a variety of genres, authored by many different talented writers.

Eastern Shore Shorts

Whether you're in the heart of the Eastern Shore or the Eastern Shore is in your heart... Characters visit familiar local restaurants, inns, shops, parks, and museums as they cross paths through the charming towns and waterways of the Eastern Shores of Maryland and Virginia.

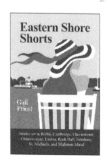

www.catandmousepress.com

Made in the USA
Middletown, DE
05 September 2019